"I di[...]

"I coul[...] [...] [...]ou
to see [...]

"I just got here. I'm sure she was too tired to stay up any longer."

"Would you like a cup?" Tessa asked.

Baffled, Morgan didn't reply.

"Of tea?" she added, holding up a mug.

"Uh, yeah. That'd be fine." His thoughts were crowded. He couldn't get the image of Tessa and Poppy out of his head. There was a…sweetness in the way she interacted with his daughter.

He'd sat in this kitchen late in the night when he couldn't sleep, but he'd always felt alone. Tessa had changed that.

She brought over the mugs, joining him at the table.

Tessa was evoking something else, something he hadn't felt since Lucy died. Startled by the thought, he jerked back his hand, overturning the cup.

She grabbed a napkin, blotting up the spilled tea.

"Sorry, let me get that." He reached for the napkin but caught her hand instead.

She froze.

Her hand was soft beneath his, and it took him a few moments to release it.

An author of thirty-six historical and contemporary romances, **Bonnie K. Winn** has won numerous awards for her *USA TODAY* and Amazon bestselling books. *Affaire de Coeur* named her one of the top ten romance authors in America. Fourteen million copies of her books have been sold worldwide. Formerly an investment executive, she shares her life with her husband as well as her son and his family, who live nearby.

Books by Bonnie K. Winn

Love Inspired

Rosewood, Texas

A Family All Her Own
Family Ties
Promise of Grace
Protected Hearts
Child of Mine
To Love Again
Lone Star Blessings
Return to Rosewood
Jingle Bell Blessings
Family by Design
Forever a Family
Falling for Her Boss

Falling for Her Boss

Bonnie K. Winn

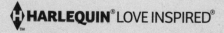

Recycling programs
for this product may
not exist in your area.

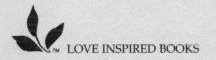 LOVE INSPIRED BOOKS

ISBN-13: 978-0-373-81849-5

Falling for Her Boss

Copyright © 2015 by Bonnie K. Winn

www.Harlequin.com

Printed in U.S.A.

Arise, my love, my fair one,
and come away;
for lo, the winter is past,
the rain is over and gone.
The flowers appear on the earth,
the time of singing has come.
—*Song of Solomon* 2:10–12

For my beautiful butterfly, Liberty.

Chapter One

Tessa Pierce crossed then recrossed her legs. For the past ten years she had been on the other side of the desk during interviews, but that wasn't the reason she was uncomfortable. Morgan Harper, owner and president of Harper Petroleum, didn't so much make her nervous, just more on edge than she'd expected. She knew the workings of oil and gas companies, how to work for a single-minded boss. Mr. Harper affected her in a different way.

"My assistant, Miss Ellis, knew exactly how I wanted things done," he was saying. "She worked for my father, then me, so she had years of experience. Retiring was—" he paused "—appropriate considering her age. But I don't have time to train someone new in every aspect of my business."

Tessa tilted her head in the direction of her résumé, laid neatly on his desk. "As you can see, I've had considerable experience in most areas of the oil and gas industry. Through its subsidiaries, Traxton has a hand in all stages of production."

Morgan didn't glance at her résumé. Tessa had the uncanny feeling that he had memorized the document. "Ten years with one employer is unusual for someone your age."

"I joined Traxton Oil right out of college. And they promote from within."

Morgan placed two fingers at one temple, indenting the skin as though trying to ward off a headache. "You've been with them this long, so why make a change?"

It was a question Tessa had prepped for and the truth had never failed her. "I want a new start because of my divorce."

His eyebrows lifted. "Houston's a pretty big place. Not enough room in it for you and your ex?"

"No," she replied simply, evenly, definitively.

He stared at her, his dark eyes appearing to bore for truth or deceit. "Cindy Mallory told me you intend to relocate to Rosewood. That the cottage that comes with the job is a big incentive. You should take into consideration that Rosewood's nothing like the city."

Her voice remained even. "That's what I'm counting on."

"If your references check out, when can you start?"

"Immediately. I've already worked my two weeks' notice."

"And if I don't hire you?"

"With my experience, someone in oil country

will. But I would enjoy having a good friend here in town. Cindy and I have known each other since we were kids. And I like what I've seen of Rosewood. Houston's invigorating, constantly busy. I'm not—" she cleared her throat "—in need of that right now."

"Bad divorce?" he asked.

Her lips tightened.

"Sorry. Not in the accepted lineup of interview questions. Then again I've never met anyone who claimed to have a good divorce, so I think I have my answer." Abruptly he stood.

Tessa stood as well, waiting for his decision.

"If we can work out an acceptable salary and employment contract, I assume you'll need some time to get moved."

"I brought the necessities. I can send for the rest of my things."

He glanced down at the calendar. "Since it's Thursday, plan to start on Monday."

So it was a yes. She exhaled, fighting the urge to slump in relief. Perfect situations weren't plentiful. And this one promised to be near ideal. Although Cindy had offered her guest room, Tessa didn't want to impose. Since the divorce, she had needed a lot of downtime. Alone time, she admitted, hating that it was true. Time when she didn't have to talk about her ex, Karl, why everything had gone so wrong. Why she was now alone.

Morgan frowned. "Do you have transportation?"

"My car," she replied.

He opened a drawer in his desk, then fished out a key. "Dorothy is my housekeeper. She'll show you to the cottage."

Holding her portfolio and purse with one hand, she extended the other.

He dropped the key into the palm of her hand. "I don't know what Cindy told you, but the cottage isn't anything elaborate. Miss Ellis was comfortable there, but I doubt it's what you're used to in Houston."

Tessa lifted her gaze, meeting his. "I'm sure it will be fine." Anything without Karl, without memories, would be welcome.

Morgan glanced at his watch. "You'll find Dorothy in the rear hall. She's expecting you."

Tessa drew her dark eyebrows together. "You were that sure I'd be right for the job?"

He neither smiled nor scowled, but she saw a flicker of disapproval in his eyes. "Dorothy is just that good."

Tessa slipped the key into her jacket pocket, then extended her hand. "I look forward to Monday."

His handshake made her swallow. Silly. She was accustomed to shaking plenty of hands during business hours. Still… Tessa turned toward the doorway of the study, trying to focus on where the rear hall would be.

Morgan watched her walk away. Efficient. That had been apparent from her résumé and the first words of her interview. He had expected her to be. Cindy and Flynn Mallory were good friends and he knew they wouldn't oversell Tessa's abilities. But something else had also been apparent. Tessa was guarded. Very guarded. He had never been divorced, but he guessed it was an ugly process. For a woman who had been very rooted in her career and life, Tessa was acting like an outlaw on the run. Cindy had unconsciously reinforced that impression when she had told him that Tessa was solid and dependable. Ten years with Traxton. No moving around.

Morgan hoped he hadn't made a hasty decision. But piles of work were growing daily. Miss Ellis had been so efficient he hadn't completely grasped how much work she took on. He rubbed his temples, wishing the headache away. He didn't want to take more aspirin. They did little to help any longer. *Get rid of the stress.* Words his doctor repeated, his parents advised, his friends cautioned. As though he could wrap up the stress and mail it away like a package.

"Daddy!" Poppy called out as she skipped through the doorway.

His expression softened. "Right here." Reaching out, he picked her up and settled her in his lap.

"Guess what?" she asked in her most dramatic four-year-old voice.

He infused his response with interest. "What?"

She leaned close, as though imparting a state secret. "There's a pretty lady in the back hall."

"Really?" he asked, managing to sound puzzled. "I have always thought Miss Dorothy was pretty."

"No, silly! Another lady!" Poppy's big blue eyes widened.

"Did you meet her?" he questioned, loving the joy Poppy found in everything.

"Nope. I hid behind the drapes. In case she wasn't 'posed to be in our house. She's all dressed up like she's going to church, the way Dorothy does."

Morgan flinched. Church wasn't a subject he ever wanted to dwell on again. "Ladies dress that way to go to work, as well."

"Miss Ellis didn't," Poppy pointed out.

No, Miss Ellis was the last of a dying breed. She had worn shirtwaist dresses to work each and every day. Unlike Tessa, who sported a chic contemporary silk suit. He guessed her dark hair was long but she had swept it up, so he couldn't be sure. Went well with her aquamarine eyes that seemed to lighten and darken at will.

Morgan pulled himself back to the child he adored. "Miss Dorothy should have your lunch ready pretty soon."

"She said I could have chocolate milk if I eat my little trees."

Morgan hid his smile. Broccoli. Dorothy cooked it at least once a week for him, as well. He didn't set a very good example, pushing it around his plate without eating a single stalk. Dorothy, being Dorothy, never gave up.

He couldn't have made it without Dorothy. His parents were already retired when Poppy's mother, Lucy, died. They had rushed home from their latest journey and had been there for him and his infant daughter. For the first three years, they had put their own dreams and plans on the back burner so they could help him care for Poppy. But he knew they longed to pursue the travels his father couldn't make when he had been running Harper Petroleum. Morgan didn't intend to let them postpone their adventures a day longer.

After they returned to their travels, he, Dorothy, her husband, Alvin, and Miss Ellis had pulled together to care for Poppy. He had tried hiring a nanny, but that had felt too impersonal. Not really knowing the woman, Morgan wasn't comfortable having her as Poppy's primary daytime caretaker. Not that his parents needed to know he'd let the nanny go. They would no doubt feel compelled to come home.

"Who is the lady?" Poppy questioned.

"She's taking Miss Ellis's job."

Poppy frowned. "Miss Ellis was real old."

And she hadn't possessed Tessa's beauty. The thought flew into his mind from left field. He hadn't cared what any woman looked like since Lucy. "That's because Miss Ellis had the job for a long time."

"Is the new lady going to get old here?"

Morgan smiled. "I don't think so."

Poppy digested this. "Can we fly my kite?"

He glanced at the pile of work on his desk. "It's almost your lunchtime, short stuff."

"Dorothy said it's in thirty hours."

Morgan did a quick mental translation. "Thirty minutes to an hour?"

She nodded, an emphatic up and down of her head. "And Dorothy said you have to come eat, too."

Considering he'd known Dorothy since she had changed his diapers, their roles of employee and employer blurred, but never in a way he minded. He hugged Poppy, then set her down. "Now, you'd better scoot."

She blew him kisses, which he caught in an upraised hand. If only all of life could be so sweet.

Tessa trailed Dorothy around the compact cottage. She hadn't expected much by Morgan's description. Pleasantly surprised by gently worn French country furniture and the terrazzo patio, she sighed.

"Something you don't like?" Dorothy asked.

"Just the opposite." Tessa turned in a semicircle. "It's so inviting. The soft colors and materials..."

"Miss Ellis wanted to redecorate. Well, back before her arthritis got so bad. Said this looked old."

Tessa lifted one shoulder. "That's part of why I like it." She touched the edge of a cabbage-rose drape. "The history. It could have been this way a century ago."

Dorothy cocked her head, indicating Tessa's slick suit, one that had fit in perfectly in downtown

Houston and definitely in the twenty-first century. "And you like that it looks old?"

"How I dress and how I like to live don't exactly match, do they?" Tessa smiled, a small smile. "I've lived with hard-edged, supermodern furniture before." Because Karl liked it. "Seemed...brittle."

Nodding, Dorothy plucked an invisible speck from a plump pillow. "When I put my feet up at night, I want them resting on something comfy. My husband, Alvin, would have a fit with glass tables and whatnot."

"I agree with Alvin." She paused. "Do you mind me asking where you and your husband live?"

"In the big house. On the main floor, past the kitchen and the butler's pantry. We have our own set of rooms. There are two other cottages on the property, but it's a lot easier on us to live in the main house. Taking care of a family isn't an eight-to-five kind of job." Dorothy plopped her hands on her hips. "Say, did you bring your overnight things?"

"I packed a small bag. I'll be sending for my clothes."

"Well, if there's anything you need, that you maybe forgot, I'm bound to have it or know how to get hold of it."

"Thank you, Dorothy."

"New job and new place to live all in one day." Dorothy shook her head. "That's a lot to take on."

Tessa firmed her chin so her lips wouldn't tremble and give her away. "It's all good."

"Even so." She hesitated. "If Morgan's a little gruff, don't let it get to you. He's been that way since… It's just his way. Well, wash up. We'll eat lunch in about twenty minutes. Casual dress."

"I'm not very hungry—"

"Need to eat something," the housekeeper insisted with a parental look that didn't invite protest.

When the door closed behind Dorothy, Tessa slipped off her jacket, then kicked off her heels. She loved the feel of her bare feet against the cool heart of pine floor.

Padding across the main room to the kitchen, she opened a cupboard and found a teapot and supplies. Loose-leaf tea, Tessa noticed with interest. Also a variety of herbal teas. The former tenant had clearly been a tea lover, as well. Having kept herself together to appear cool and collected for the interview, Tessa felt drained. It was difficult to appear upbeat and enthusiastic when she wanted to crawl under the covers and never come out. A hot cup of herbal tea and the comfortable-looking chair near the window seemed like a perfect way to lift her spirits.

She had hoped to escape lunch with her new boss, but at least she could cut the meal short, using the valid excuse that she needed to send for her belongings. They wouldn't amount to much. Karl could keep the furniture in their condo. She had taken the precaution of packing her sentimental items and bringing them along. Clothes could be repurchased, but good memories were irreplaceable. But how many good memories did she really have connected with her marriage? Few, she now realized. And even those were single-sided.

After a quick call to Cindy to let her know she'd gotten the job, Tessa enjoyed a cup of tea. Sighing, she knew she had to change for lunch. She truly wasn't hungry, but didn't want to offend Morgan or Dorothy.

Opening her bag, she retrieved a pair of jeans and a cotton blouse. Glancing in the mirror, even she could see the fatigue traced through her expression. Eyes now constantly dry from crying herself to sleep looked red and raw. It was a wonder she had gotten the job. She rummaged in her makeup bag and found the eye drops. Some fresh blusher and lipstick helped a bit.

She just had to remember to keep upbeat, to squash the unhappy note that colored her voice these days. Tessa leaned closer to the mirror. "You're a mess, you know. Perk up." She probably should have chosen coffee instead of herbal tea for the caffeine pickup. Too late now.

Tessa decided she preferred entering the big house through the kitchen rather than ringing the bell at the set of big doors in the front. It was the route Dorothy had taken them to the cottage. She knocked lightly. A small child appeared in the doorway.

Not expecting her, Tessa drew in her breath. "Ah. Hello. I'm Tessa. Dorothy is expecting me for lunch."

"Daddy, too," the poppet replied, holding a well-used stuffed dog in one hand, staring intently at Tessa.

"Yes." Tessa paused, remembering what Cindy had said about the motherless child. "I'm going to be working for him."

"But not like Miss Ellis," the girl informed her.

"No?"

The child shook her head. "Miss Ellis got old here and you aren't going to."

"Okay, Poppy, that'll be enough," Dorothy said, coming up behind them in time to hear the child's last remark.

"But Daddy said—"

"We don't repeat what others say, do we? Now, wash up and we'll start lunch." Dorothy lifted her gaze. "Morgan's having a plate in his study. He tends to…focus on his work. But we're still glad to have you join us."

"I don't want to be any trouble," Tessa reminded her. "I'm not that hungry."

"Then hopefully, you'll appreciate a simple meal. I made sliders."

Tessa raised her eyebrows, thinking the term was a progressive reference, one she hadn't expected.

Dorothy reached for a dish towel. "Now, I know they're just small hamburgers, but Poppy had them at lunch in Houston with her dad and thought they were so much better than full-size hamburgers." Dorothy rolled her eyes. "So, now we have lots of *little* burgers. I made a salad in case you eat healthy. I sneak veggies in, too."

"Sounds good. I don't have any dietary restrictions. I suppose I should, but I pretty much eat what I like. Then I run or walk long enough every day to burn some of it off."

Dorothy's eyes were observant but kind. "Doesn't look like you need to."

Tessa had lost weight unintentionally since the separation and divorce. These days nothing perked her appetite. But she didn't want to seem ungrateful.

"Can I sit next to you?" Poppy was asking, having returned to gaze up at her intently.

"If it's all right with Dorothy," Tessa replied, swimming in uncertain waters.

"Lunch is always casual," Dorothy replied. "Unless it's some *do*, which we haven't had in a long time."

"I saw you all dressed pretty," Poppy chimed in. "Before."

The child must have silently darted in and out earlier. Tessa was certain she wouldn't have forgotten this little one. Poppy smiled, dimpling her cherubic face. "Can I sit by you?" she asked again.

Tessa melted. What a little charmer.

Dorothy deftly changed the positions of the settings so that they were side by side rather than across the table from one another.

Tessa noticed only the two plates. "Aren't you and your husband having lunch, too?"

Shaking her head, Dorothy placed a colorful bowl of salad on the table. "Alvin's in town running some errands. Probably sounds silly, but I'll eat with him when he gets back. After being married over forty years, I'm used to seeing his face across the table from me."

Incredibly sweet. The kind of future Tessa had always envisioned for herself. "I...I think it's nice."

"Poppy and I are going to make chocolate-chip bars after lunch. Be good for dessert when Alvin and I eat."

"I get to mix 'em," Poppy told her. "And the most bestest part—put the chocolate in the bowl."

"A few of the chips always take a detour," Dorothy admitted cheerfully.

Poppy smiled brightly, huge blue eyes staring up at her, unblinking.

If she and Karl had adopted, it was possible she would have a child just Poppy's age by now. Tessa swallowed the growing lump in her throat.

Cindy had told her that Poppy's mother died when she was only a few days old. Fate could be cruel. Here she sat, next to a child who would never know her mother, while Tessa herself would never have a daughter.

Damaged. The word was like a curse, blanketing her in desperate pain. Had Lucy Harper been similarly cursed? Because, for the life of her, Tessa couldn't understand why their places hadn't been exchanged. All of her own dreams had been filled with a husband and family. And for a few fleeting days, Lucy Harper had had that. Now, Tessa was sitting next to the beautiful child and silent wishes stirred the air, pierced her heart.

Just then Poppy touched her hand. Baby soft and sweet. And Tessa made herself smile, wondering if her smile would ever inwardly blossom again.

Chapter Two

Early Monday morning, Morgan studied the lengthy contract. His attorney would examine the legal wording, but Morgan had to be certain the terms profited Harper Petroleum. Big oil was still big business in Texas. And along with oil came petroleum transportation companies that were huge in comparison to his own operation. Harper was one of the few independents left not swallowed up by the deep pockets of corporate greed. And even though his company's size made it challenging for him to stay competitive, he was determined to remain independent.

Morgan knew the names of all his drivers, gaugers, mechanics, hub and office staff. He'd never viewed them as a lump of people. Each was an individual. Nearly all had families depending on them. And all depended on Harper Petroleum for their jobs. While his company wasn't a nonprofit, it had never undercut salaries to ratchet up the profit margin. He knew that wasn't the case with a lot of his competitors.

With the exception of Poppy, the past four years had been a nightmare. Every day, it was a struggle to keep his head above water in the cutthroat business, while balancing home and work. He never wanted to shortchange his daughter, which was why he spent so many days working from home. There had always been a fully equipped office at the house, dating back to when his grandfather had been at the helm. But it had been used only when necessary, not as a routine practice. The offices in town, needed to impress clients, were still kept up. Entering them, no one would detect that he wasn't often in residence.

The aching in his head increased. *Try to forget, to let go.* Advice that he neither asked for nor wanted was offered on a continual basis. Lifelong friends thought he should compartmentalize his feelings, allowing his love for Poppy to flow while at the same time shutting off his continuing love and grief for his late wife. His daughter was a miniature replica of her mother. Lucy would have adored her beautiful, winsome child. He could imagine the twin sets of matching eyes that twinkled, mouths that would burst with laughter.

But there had been no laughter within him since she died. Well…with the exception of when he was with Poppy. She could coax a smile from him when he was certain his heart had turned to stone. And, along with the love, he had developed a protective streak that was near manic.

He hadn't told Tessa, but he'd run a full background check on her prior to the interview. Initially, everyone who worked at the house full-time and part-time had been with the Harper family for years and could be trusted. Since Poppy's birth, every new hire, regardless of position, went through the same background check.

Miss Ellis had told him he was overreacting, but that was what he'd been told when he had seen the first signs in Lucy's eyes that something was wrong. Of course she was tired, the doctor had assured him. Brand-new mothers were exhausted. But Lucy wasn't simply tired. The aneurism that had blasted through her brain was sudden and final.

He hadn't believed it at first. God wouldn't be that cruel. Give with one hand and grab with the other fist. Lucy had been one of the kindest people in the world. Her death just didn't make sense in any possible way. There was no lesson to learn, no grievance that had been satisfied. No, his beautiful wife had been snatched away just when her dearest dream, a baby, had come into her life.

A light knock on the study door startled him. He whirled around, eyebrows drawn downward, his mouth forming a ferocious frown. "What?"

"Excuse me, Mr. Harper," Tessa began tentatively. "You didn't say what time you wanted to begin today. I can come back if you're busy."

"No!" Realizing he had barked at her, Morgan made himself breathe, push the past away for the moment. "I have a contract for you to study. And it's Morgan."

"Fine." She hesitated. "Can I bring you some coffee? Since it's early?"

"Early?" Belatedly he realized she didn't know he hadn't slept, that he'd worked deep into the night, then progressed into the world of memories. He glanced out the windows at the weak fingers of first morning light. "You don't have to begin this early."

"I couldn't sleep," she confessed. "I ran out of coffee in the cottage and thought I'd see if I could borrow a cup. I didn't think to ask where the grocery store in town is."

"Dorothy's up before the sun," Morgan replied. "And she'll have coffee brewing."

"She does." Tessa held up her steaming mug.

"Of course, you saw her when you came in." He smoothed the deepening ridge in his forehead.

"I've seen her up early every morning since I've been here."

"Which means you've been up early, as well."

His comment made her look uncomfortable. "Just restless in a new place."

"Everything okay?"

She stiffened. "What do you mean?"

"The cottage. Is it all right?"

Again she was discomfited. "Yes—fine, I mean."

"Don't let me keep you," he said as he turned toward his computer screen.

"Keep?"

"Your coffee," he reminded her.

"I don't know what you take in yours," she queried.

"A touch of sugar. But you don't have to bring me coffee. I hired you for your brains, not to be my personal assistant."

"I'm going to get more coffee anyway," she replied, "and I never mind bringing back an extra. It's not as though I'm stepping and fetching."

After she left, Morgan ran one hand over his disheveled hair. He could imagine what she'd thought of his rumpled appearance. She, on the other hand, looked perfectly polished, dressed in a deceptively simple dress that he was certain cost more than most administrative employees could afford. Perhaps she had done well in her divorce settlement.

Then again, she had been making good money at Traxton. Rather extraordinary that she would leave them after ten years just to get away from her ex.

Houston, a sprawling giant, could almost guarantee there would be no chance meetings. Unless her ex-husband had also worked at Traxton. Even so, she could have found work in Houston's Energy Corridor or downtown. Something more had sent her scuttling all the way to Rosewood.

Must have been some divorce. Even though she hadn't divulged the details, it had clearly been a bad experience. A flash of familiar pain traced through his gut. He couldn't understand how anyone could throw away a marriage. What he would give to have his late wife back…

Tessa's footsteps were light on the pine floor, then virtually noiseless on the thick woven silk rug that padded the room. The decor hadn't changed much since his father's day, even his grandfather's day. A massive mahogany desk dominated the space. And his leather chair was worn in just the way Morgan liked it.

A wall of built-in bookcases held everything from a dictionary to volumes of law regarding royalty rights for the oil. Most people didn't know it was the transportation company that calculated and paid landowners their portion of the oil revenue. Harper had an entire department devoted to that duty.

"Dorothy said I should use china cups," Tessa told him as she carefully set his coffee on the desk.

"My mother insisted on using the good dishes every day. Said if they were appropriate for company, they were appropriate for us, too."

Tessa chuckled. "I'm afraid I'd have a collection of chips, cracks and pieces if I followed that policy."

"We do. Every now and then we have to buy replacements. Dorothy keeps up with them." Morgan mentally dismissed the less than stimulating subject, refocusing on work. "All of the state reports are up-to-date—barely. It's the third week of the month and they'll be due on the first."

Tessa nodded, transitioning smoothly between

the unrelated subjects. "Is the computer on my desk networked with yours?"

"Yes. I've written down your password. It's in the top middle drawer. Familiarize yourself with the setup, then we can go over questions."

"And the report you want me to study?"

"Front and center on top of your desk."

"All right, then."

Work had never intimidated her. But she had taken her advancements one rung at a time, building on what she learned in each position. She'd never vaulted to the top man's office in one giant leap. But this wasn't the time to become faint of heart.

Near the end of her first week, Tessa found the work challenging but she was learning everything she could about Harper. The morning disappeared one computer screen after another. Tessa didn't realize it was lunchtime until a small hand tugged persistently on her sleeve. Poppy waited to be recognized.

Tessa smiled at the child's serious expression. "Well, hello." She noticed a stuffed dog in the child's hand, remembering she had seen it on her first day. "And who's this?"

"Freckles," Poppy replied seriously. "He's my best friend."

If true, that was terribly sad. "He looks like a fine friend."

"Dorothy says it's time for lunch."

Automatically, Tessa lifted her wrist, glancing at her watch. "So it is. Have you told your dad?"

"Daddy's not here."

Hiding her frown, Tessa wondered why he hadn't let her know he was going out. Fielding phone calls would be more effective if she knew when he wasn't available. A second frown settled between her eyebrows. The phone hadn't rung all morning. Leaning forward, she checked the digital readout, which said all calls had been forwarded to the main office for the day. Morgan Harper was proving to be a difficult study. Evidently he felt he'd taken care of what was necessary. Accustomed to being her boss's right hand, it was unsettling to see how self-sufficient this particular boss was.

"Are you coming?" Poppy questioned.

Sensing a touch of uncertainty in the child, Tessa grinned widely. "Can't keep me away. Do you know what we're having?"

"Fried catfish and chocolate pudding."

"That's quite a combination," Tessa managed to reply without giving away her amusement. "What's your favorite part?"

"Pudding," Poppy replied without hesitation.

"Mine probably will be, too," Tessa confided.

The kitchen was homey, warm, filled with the quiet current of voices. Dorothy and Alvin stood by the sink, shoulders leaned in, touching. Just a simple gesture, but it told of a deep connection.

"Can I do anything to help?" Tessa offered.

Dorothy turned her head. "Everything's already done. It's nothing fancy, not like what you're used to in the city."

Tessa laughed without mirth. "I practically live on coffee when I'm working, so you're right, this isn't what I'm used to." She sniffed the enticing aroma of freshly cooked fish, but she still couldn't work up an appetite.

Four place settings were on the table. Dorothy inclined her head in their direction. "When we eat in the kitchen we keep it casual."

Tessa interpreted that to mean when Morgan didn't join them. She wondered if he ever got lonely eating on his own. Silly thought, she chastised herself. Men who ran entire companies didn't lack for company.

Fresh iced tea filled the glasses and a large bowl of crisp salad sat beside the platter of fish. Local catfish, Alvin had informed her.

"Store-bought rolls," Dorothy muttered. "Means I'm getting old. Never used to buy them, always made my own."

"I like bakeries," Tessa confessed. She used to love buying pastries on weekend mornings to share with Karl. Seemed ridiculous that she had believed all was fine in those days.

Alvin dried his hands. "Dorothy makes the best bread in the county. Won the blue ribbon for that and her cinnamon rolls five years straight at the county fair. But the town bakery's okay. They bake fresh every day."

Dorothy looked a tad embarrassed at the praise. "Poppy likes their cookies. They make all kinds of fancy cartoon shapes."

"But Dorothy's taste goodest," Poppy declared. "And she lets me help."

"You're probably the best part," Tessa told her as they shared a smile.

The back door opened and they all turned toward it. Morgan entered, his unguarded face weary.

"Daddy!" Poppy exclaimed happily.

For a moment pure love eclipsed the fatigue in Morgan's face. "Hey, you."

Hopping down, she ran to him, visibly delighted when he swept her up and nuzzled her cheek. "How's my girl?"

"Hungry," she replied cheerfully. Then she leaned even closer. "And we're having pudding," she added in a loud whisper.

He pretended delighted surprise. "But what will we have for dessert?"

"Oh, Daddy!" She giggled and he swung her up again.

Morgan looked reluctant when he set her back down.

But Poppy immediately tugged at his hand, chasing away any possibility of escape. "You have to sit by me."

Just then he looked up, seeming to notice Tessa

for the first time. Unconsciously she straightened, then smiled tentatively.

His gaze gave nothing away and she couldn't tell if he was displeased by her presence. No one had mentioned whether she would be taking her lunches with the family. Dorothy had insisted the first day and she had continued coming to the kitchen for lunch, but now Tessa wondered if she was intruding. Standing, she pushed back her chair.

"Where are you going?" Morgan asked.

"Well, you're here now and I know Poppy wants to sit with you and—"

"There's plenty of room and from what I hear, plenty of pudding." He reached into a cabinet and pulled out a plate. Dorothy had already collected another setting of silverware.

"You can sit by Daddy, too," Poppy informed her. "I get to sit on this side." The child indicated her favorite spot.

Tessa felt like the last pickling cucumber being shoved into an overstuffed jar. Not that the table was small, but it had already been set up to serve four. An extra setting put it out of balance. The thought barely formed when Poppy tugged Morgan to the middle seat between herself and Tessa.

Proximity immediately changed. Tiny Poppy hadn't taken up much space in her chair. But Morgan, tall with broad shoulders, filled the area. Tessa hugged her elbows to her sides, trying to minimize contact. Instead of making her less visible, her tactic caused Morgan to glance her way. Feeling like a fool, she straightened again, accidentally brushing her arm against his. Startled, she almost withdrew, reconsidered and tried to look unaffected. Glancing across the table at Dorothy and Alvin, Tessa immediately saw from their expressions that she had failed miserably.

"Pudding?" Morgan asked, extending the salad bowl. He leaned close, his voice low. "Poppy has decreed all courses include pudding."

"I...I love pudding." Tessa sought to make her voice sound bright as she reached for the tongs.

He looked at the tiny serving she scooped out and frowned. "Not your favorite flavor?"

"I want to save room for all the courses," she improvised, knowing she wouldn't finish even the small amount of food she would put on her plate.

To her relief, Morgan didn't pursue it, instead turning to his daughter. "Extra olives?"

"Yes, please."

He carefully plucked a generous helping of black olives from the bowl along with a portion of the greens and tomatoes. Tessa guessed Dorothy had loaded the salad with Poppy's favorites.

She wasn't sure how or why, but Morgan's presence had changed the entire dynamic of their little gathering. Poppy was aglow, her connection to Morgan deep and visible. Alvin and Dorothy seemed more content somehow. And she...she wasn't sure what she was. It was no longer easy and light. Tessa realized she was being silly, that she had eaten more business lunches with employers than she could count. No need to be nervous.

"Daddy, you promised to take me to ride Corn-flake," Poppy pleaded.

Morgan paused, his fork midair. "Today?"

The child's head bobbed up and down as though attached to a string.

Tessa was tempted to offer to cover for him for the afternoon if he needed the time with his daughter, but she wasn't sure how the gesture would be taken. And, in truth, she didn't know enough about Harper Petroleum to cover for him.

Morgan glanced her way. "Cornflake is Poppy's pony."

"Ah," she replied, picturing the cute child on an equally cute pony.

"All work and no play," Dorothy mused, passing the platter of fish.

The forces had gathered. Graciously, Morgan bowed to them. "After lunch. That doesn't mean we skip the fish, either."

Poppy's face crinkled, her plan apparently quashed.

Tessa couldn't suppress her own smile as she imagined Poppy bolting her pudding, then tearing upstairs to change into riding gear.

Morgan caught her eye, apparently interpreting her smile. "Experience," he explained succinctly.

Poppy practically danced in her chair as she gob-bled down her lunch. Tessa wondered if their outings were that rare or if she was just excited. A glance that morning at the company's structural chart had indicated that Morgan carried the bulk of the executive load. There wasn't a tier of vice presidents to allocate the work to. Despite having help at home, he was a single parent. One she guessed spent a great deal of time working if what she'd seen so far was any indication.

In record time, Poppy finished her lunch. "May I be excused?" she asked breathlessly, already sliding off her chair.

"Yes."

Grabbing her stuffed dog, the child ran from the room, her shoes clattering as she crossed the entry hall and reached the staircase.

Morgan pulled out his cell phone, checked his missed calls, then sighed.

"Anything I can do to help?" Tessa questioned, now that Poppy was gone.

He shook his head. "Even if you'd been here long enough to know these people, they're calls I have to deal with myself."

"Don't you have another executive who can handle some of your duties?" she questioned, hoping she wasn't crossing a line.

"No."

"And he should," Dorothy chimed in, tipping the pitcher, refilling glasses.

Morgan shot the housekeeper a look that might scorch the skin off some, but she remained unperturbed. He laid his napkin on the table. "I'm going to change. Tessa, I assume you noticed that the calls are rerouted today. When I get back from the ride, we can go over the state reports."

She nodded. "I hope you and Poppy have a good time."

His gaze was reflective. "No need for you to worry. Poppy's my concern."

Tessa tried not to take offense. He was her boss, not a friend. He was right. His personal life wasn't her concern. But she'd never worked in a situation quite like this one. An office in his home, her cottage on his property. It was a major change from working for a big corporation. Then again, everything in her life was changing. She'd never thought she would leave her hometown. Her marriage was supposed to last forever. And children...they were supposed to be part of her future. How would it be to have a lovely girl like Poppy to spend the afternoon with? One whose face lit with love when she spotted her parent?

Tessa blindly turned her attention back to her plate, not seeing what it contained, not caring. There was no hint of tears. When Karl had tossed her away, she'd cried until all her tears were gone. Instead, there was emptiness, a great cavern nothing would ever fill. It was only in the dark of night, when she should be sleeping, that the tears dampened her pillow, refusing to remain inside.

Morgan spoke quietly with Dorothy and Alvin,

their voices filling in the silence Tessa isolated herself in. She had accepted that her life had changed, had embraced the finality of moving away from Karl. But in her plans for building a new life for herself, she hadn't counted on missing one essential factor: hope in the future. Because from where she sat, that seemed unbearably bleak.

Morgan watched Poppy skip toward the house, her short legs lifting in the early-evening dusk. He had planned to keep the outing short, but Poppy had been so taken with Cornflake that they'd extended the ride. She even elicited a promise from him that he would take her to ride Cornflake every week.

Dorothy had been nagging him to spend more time with Poppy. So when she pleaded for ice cream he gave in. One delicious but messy cone later, she had insisted that she was still hungry. So, he'd caved and they ate dinner at the café. Poppy loved going out. Anywhere, anytime. His parents had catered to her, taking her with them constantly. He didn't have that luxury. Too many employees were counting on him to keep Harper solvent, to make sure their jobs were safe.

Cutting through the side lawn, he paused, glancing ahead. Tessa walked slowly away from her cottage. He wondered where she was headed. His property line extended a good distance. His great-grandparents had purchased the property as acreage that amounted to four large city lots. One of the cottages was their original home before the big house had been built. His great-grandfather had been a pipeline gauger, then an oil lease hound, taking a small investment and making it grow. The generations that followed kept building the business. During those years, a larger house had been needed to entertain clients.

And the cottages were handy, he thought, watching Tessa through the gauzy twilight. Her hair was definitely long. No longer neatly pinned up, the dark strands tumbled past her shoulders. She had changed from her stylish suit to a long cottony-looking dress. Aquamarine, he decided, squinting in the dimming light. The color of her eyes, he remembered. Funny the details that stuck out in his memory.

Tessa turned just then as though sensing someone watching. But the low-hanging branches of a crepe myrtle camouflaged his presence. As she tipped her face up, the dying light of the day's sun silhouetted her features. The picture solidified in his thoughts as he drew in a breath. And he suspected the image wouldn't soon fade.

Chapter Three

Days, then weeks toddled by as Tessa kept upping her learning curve. By her fourth week, she had grasped two things—the rudimentary elements of Harper Petroleum and the fact that Morgan didn't spend enough time with his daughter. He rarely made it to family meals. And he was out of town often, meeting with his field supervisors and contractors and performing various other tasks Tessa believed he could turn over to someone else. She understood the current thinking—that middle management was an unnecessary drain on the company's financial resources—but Morgan needed help. She hadn't met all the office staff, but surely he employed someone either in the field or office whom he could promote, then delegate some of his work.

Dorothy let Morgan know that he needed to be home more often, but he didn't change his behavior. Today was the first Saturday Tessa hadn't worked. Morgan had gone to Jefferson in East Texas to check on a new pipeline installation.

Fortunately her friend Cindy Mallory had a free day. Her husband, Flynn, had taken all their kids to the skating rink. And Cindy insisted a girls' day out was exactly what she needed.

"How are you settling in?" Cindy asked, picking up a shoe, turning it around to inspect the heel.

"Fine."

Cindy raised one eyebrow. "How's Morgan as a boss?"

"Fine."

"We aren't going to get far with this line of questioning if you stick to one-word answers." Cindy smiled. "Spill. What do you think of the job?"

"I think I like it."

"Think?"

"It's different working for one man instead of a corporation and there's the proximity to his home, the office in his house." Tessa thought of all that was new in her life. "I like the cottage. And, in ways, it's comforting to know there are people nearby."

"But?"

"Not exactly a *but*. Just that I'm treading on a lot of undefined territory. I don't want to offend Dorothy by not eating lunch with them. On the other hand, I don't want Morgan to feel that I'm intruding."

"I think the world of Morgan, but he isn't exactly restrained when it comes to giving his opinion. He wouldn't hesitate to let you know if you were crossing a line."

Tessa stared at a pair of navy shoes. "Does it

worry you that Morgan doesn't spend enough time with Poppy?"

Cindy stopped in her tracks, throwing back her gleaming red hair as she spun around. "Where did that come from?"

"Just that Morgan spends all of his time working. Since I've been here, he's only taken Poppy out once even though he promised he'd take her to ride her horse every week."

Frowning, Cindy paused. "Morgan adores her."

"Oh, I can see that. And it's mutual. But, not having a mother, it seems that Poppy needs extra parent time, not less." Tessa replaced the navy shoe without having really looked at it. "I know I don't have kids, so it's not as though I'm an expert."

"That's not what I'm questioning." Cindy looked perplexed. "Just that Morgan's devoted to Poppy."

"I think so, too, but that doesn't stop her from being lonely. The poor kid even hangs around me when I'm working. Dorothy and Alvin give her all the attention they can, but they're busy taking care of the house and grounds."

Cindy cleared her throat. "Does it…bother you? Having Poppy around, I mean."

"Just because I can't have one of my own doesn't mean I've gone off children. I'm just worried that she's getting the short end of the stick." Tessa rubbed her forehead. "This really isn't any of my business. Morgan's my employer, not a friend."

"There's nothing wrong with caring," Cindy reminded her gently, her calm voice belying the crop of flame-colored hair that framed her face.

"If I had a daughter like Poppy…" Tessa shook her head. "Do you think I'm being judgmental because I'm jealous?"

"Are you feeling jealous?"

"I don't think so." Tessa thought of the sweet child. "What I keep feeling is the irony. Poppy's mother had everything to live for and…"

"You don't?" Cindy put a comforting hand on Tessa's elbow. "Just because Karl's a jerk doesn't mean you won't have a full future with everything you want in it."

"Because there are so many men out there who want to marry a woman who can't bear his children."

"I want to believe that sort of thinking is in the past, Tessa. You just have to pick the right man."

"I thought I had," Tessa replied dully. "And since I'm so good at picking them, we should have every confidence that I can find another winner."

"Give it time. I never believed Flynn would come around. I still marvel that he ever did."

Flynn had fallen in love with Cindy's sister, Julia. They had married and were raising their triplets when Julia had died. It was a blow that shattered them all. Lacking any other family, Flynn had moved with his daughters to Rosewood so that Cindy could be in their lives.

Ironically, Cindy had initially moved to Rosewood to escape Flynn and her continued feelings for him.

Cindy had met him first, fallen in love with him first, but Flynn had chosen Julia, the steady, responsible sister. It took time, faith and a depth of love to learn that Flynn had made that choice because of his family background and pain-filled past.

Once she had unraveled Flynn's past, Cindy was able to understand what Flynn needed. Now they were raising a family together, and their love had only deepened over the years. But she could remember being on the outside as Tessa was now. How alone and unloved she'd felt.

"You and Flynn are perfect together," Tessa was saying. "Your family...well, it's perfect, too."

"Now," Cindy reminded her.

Tessa remembered all that Cindy had gone through, how difficult it had been for her to uproot her entire life in Houston and move away. She'd left behind the only family she had along with all her friends. At least Tessa had her family. Her parents lived close to Houston, but they were still in her life.

They had been supportive when Karl ended the marriage. Her parents hadn't been thrilled that she'd chosen to relocate but tried to understand. Like most people, they thought Houston was big enough for her to avoid her ex-husband. But they liked Cindy and knew she would be a good anchor. Her father had extracted a promise that she would return to Houston if things didn't work out in Rosewood, if she wasn't happy.

Happy. A funny term. One she had taken for

granted most of her life. She'd always felt pretty blessed. With her family, her job, finding a man she thought she could share her life with…

Cindy turned from the shoes. "I don't know about you, but I could use a cup of tea."

Tessa didn't care about shoe shopping. She was really only tagging along. "Sounds good."

"We'll go to Maddie's, the place I told you about."

"The Tea House?"

"Tea Cart. But yes. Best tea in the world. Maddie mixes her own blends. And her lemon bars are to die for. She makes them with real shortbread."

Still not having much of an appetite, Tessa nodded. "I do love tea."

"I know."

"Cindy, I'm sorry. I'm being a real downer. You've given up a Saturday and I'm about as much fun as a rain-soaked picnic."

Cindy smiled. "I didn't come out today to paint the town. I'm fine with having a low-key day. It's great having you live so close again. I've missed you. You're going to love Maddie. She's a native to Rosewood. And she's an inspiration. Takes care of her mother, who has dementia, and she has become a great mother to her husband's niece."

Tessa shook her head. "You don't see it, do you? *You're* an inspiration, Cindy."

Predictably, Cindy protested. "Just living my life."

"Which includes supporting and sponsoring the Children's Home, raising *your* three nieces, adopting a parentless child, raising your own children, being a great friend..."

Embarrassed, Cindy's ivory cheeks reddened. "Stop that. You make it sound like more than it is."

"Afraid not. But I am happy about finding a new place for tea. Does she sell any of her blends?"

"Yes! I have three favorites, couldn't pick just one." Cindy opened the door and they stepped out onto the sidewalk. "Typical. We love things in threes."

After college Tessa and Cindy had reconnected over tea. Both had been invited to a luncheon for women in the oil industry. Tessa had been new to Traxton, and Cindy was representing her family business. Squeezed together at one of the last tables, they had caught up over a pot of spiced orange pekoe. College had taken them in opposite directions. Destiny brought them back together.

Ironic that Rosewood had become a sanctuary for them both. Right now Tessa didn't relish the thought of returning to Houston, something that worried her parents.

As though reading her thoughts, Cindy asked about them.

"They just want me to be happy," she summed up, thinking she would have to invite them for a visit when she could handle it. The thought of entertaining anyone, even her parents, was exhausting.

"Natural." Cindy hesitated. "If you'd like, I could invite them for a weekend."

"The cottage has a spare bedroom." Tessa took a deep breath. "I know you're just trying to help, but I'm not quite ready for a weekend visit." Especially because some days it was difficult just to breathe, to force herself to go to work, to interact with anyone.

"I remember days of curling up in bed, wishing the world would go away." Cindy's eyes darkened in reflection. "I just want to help."

"This—" Tessa snagged her friend's elbow "—this, spending time with me even though I'm not fun. It's helping…more than I can tell you."

Cindy squeezed Tessa's hand in return. "Fun isn't a friendship requirement. I don't remember being much fun several years ago. But that didn't stop you from being there for me."

"It was all a plan so I could disappear from Houston." Tessa dredged up a laugh. "And to find a new tea source."

"That I can promise." They had reached the Tea Cart. "And after today you'll wonder how you lived this long without Maddie's specialties."

Meeting Maddie, Tessa tried to relax.

"I hope you'll come here often," Maddie told her.

The bell over the door jangled. Being Saturday, the shop was busy. They found a table by the window, affording a view of Main Street. Tessa had immediately taken to the Victorian town that still looked as though horse-drawn carriages could travel its cobblestone streets. Thriving businesses populated the original buildings. Unlike so many towns that had dried up because of a superstore's dominance or that catered strictly to tourism, Rosewood maintained its own identity. On the sidewalk directly outside, café tables sat beneath a canopy of aged trees and nineteenth-century streetlamps.

A few young couples sat at these tiny tables, absorbed in each other. Just as young love, any love, should, Tessa realized. Had she and Karl ever stared at each other with such devotion?

It wasn't something she remembered. Why hadn't she noticed that back then? Had she really not paid attention to the details of her marriage? It was one of the questions that itched in her thoughts, robbed her of sleep, resonated in her loneliness.

"How do you like your tea?" Cindy asked.

Tessa pushed away the nagging thoughts and picked up her cup to taste. Surprisingly, the effect was immediately piquant. She took another sip. "This really is good."

"I knew you'd like it." Cindy put her own cup in a saucer. "It doesn't seem like it today, but the time will come when little things like this will make you smile again."

Tessa didn't think they would.

"I know you don't think so right now," Cindy continued, echoing Tessa's thoughts. "But I wouldn't try to convince you if I didn't believe it." Her cell phone rang and she glanced at the screen. "Sorry. I have to take this."

Tessa sipped her tea while trying not to listen, but she couldn't miss the distress in her friend's voice.

"Something wrong?" Tessa asked as Cindy clicked the phone off.

"An inconvenience really." Cindy's face filled with regret. "It's the Children's Home," she began, referring to the organization she had founded that fostered children. She had established the home as an outgrowth of a class she taught at church. It all began with one unwanted child, which led to forming the Rainbow class for kids who needed extra attention. The group had grown, then taken on a life of its own. Cindy's house had been adapted as a permanent home for children without homes of their own.

"Something you need to take care of now?" Sensing her friend was feeling bad because their outing was about to be cut short, Tessa made an impulsive offer. "What if I come with you? That is, if I can help at all."

Cindy's face brightened in an instant. "What a wonderful idea! I'm sorry to cut our tea short, but the kitchen at the home is stocked with Maddie's goodies, so I can brew us a pot of fresh tea. I make a run at least twice a week." She reached for her purse and pulled out some cash. "This is mine."

Seeing how pleased her friend was at the offer to join her, Tessa swallowed the regret her impulse was now causing. Surely she could take herself out of her own worries to help. Feeling ashamed of herself for the regret, she picked up her own purse.

Cindy left a generous tip on the table. She acted so naturally that Tessa often forgot that Cindy came from wealth. As they drove toward what had once been Cindy's home, Tessa guessed much of her inheritance had been spent on the children she took in.

It didn't take long to reach the neighborhood, which was just on the perimeter of Main Street in one of the oldest areas in the town. The house was an aged Victorian that wore its years well. Tessa could picture Cindy at home here, taking on a dozen tasks as she was wont to do.

Children spilled out of the doorway like errant sunbeams. Tessa felt the tugging ache of knowing none would ever be hers. As a single woman, she understood the difficulty of adoption, reluctantly acknowledging that if possible every child deserved two parents. Certainly more than a lone parent who worked sixty-plus hours a week.

However, it was nearly impossible to hold on to the pain as children rushed toward them, toward Cindy.

"So many smiles!" Cindy greeted them. "Saturday smiles?"

"Miss Cindy!" the voices chorused. Several hands tugged at hers. Tessa swallowed, wondering at these little ones who were so fond of her friend.

The door stood open and slowly they traveled up the walk and inside. It was impossible to hurry with so many little bodies pressed close.

"Who wants to run and get Miss Donna?" Cindy asked them.

"Me, me!" was shouted as several headed toward the kitchen.

"Do they all live here?" Tessa asked when there was a semiquiet moment.

"No. Some are here for the day. It's one of our programs to help single and/or working parents. And the full-time residents enjoy the company." Cindy hung her purse on a tall coatrack in the hall.

Tessa followed suit, noticing the exquisite detail in the moldings and woodwork. The floor appeared to be made of rare longleaf Texas pine. "This is just as pretty as you told me."

"You should have come and visited while I lived here," Cindy replied. "It made a wonderful home."

"Do you miss it?"

"Not really. I still see it so often. And my heart is with Flynn and the kids. Wouldn't matter if we lived in a bamboo hut. Wherever they are, it's home."

Genuinely glad for her friend's happiness, Tessa didn't feel any envy. Just puzzlement. Why did some people get it so right the first time?

Cindy caught her gaze. "Something heavy weighing on your mind?"

"Didn't realize I was so transparent. Just wondering how some people choose the right person first time around."

"If you're thinking of me, remember I was on a very twisted path for a very long time." Cindy's green eyes darkened. "I was basically in love with what should have been the worst person possible— my sister's husband. I can remember that feeling of wondering if I'd ever be part of a couple. Seemed as though the whole world had paired off. Except for me. To me it looked as though I was going to have a lifetime of being alone. Don't compare yourself, Tessa. Your situation is unique. *You* are unique. And that's a good thing. I don't know why the Lord has given you this challenge. I don't know why He gave me mine, but I trust it's for the best. Mine has turned out to be."

"My faith isn't in question," Tessa replied quietly.

"Of course not! But sometimes it's hard not to question what happens. I did."

Uncertainty seized her. "You did?"

"Constantly." Cindy's eyes were steady. "I couldn't understand why the Lord wanted me to be alone, to love someone I couldn't have."

"You never said…"

"It seemed so wrong. Julia was happy. I loved her. I didn't want to do anything to change her happiness. But I couldn't get Flynn out of my heart."

Tessa nodded, remembering the sweetness of her own romance when she was young. "Karl seemed so different at first. I never dreamed…"

"Which is why you can't stop dreaming. I don't think you have to marry to be happy, but I do think the Lord has someone for you."

"Hiding in plain sight?" Tessa tried to joke.

The determination in Cindy's gaze didn't waver. "Just might be."

Sounding like a thousand little footsteps, the kids returned. Cindy reached down to pick up the shortest child.

"This little sweetheart is Sandy."

"Hi, Sandy."

The little girl looked at Tessa steadily. "Who are you?"

Surprised at the child's grasp on language, Tessa smiled. "Wow. How old are you?"

"Four."

"We've had some challenges, didn't we, Sandy?" Cindy responded, giving the child a hug.

Challenges that had stunted her growth, no doubt. She looked no more than two at the most. Tessa swallowed, wondering if the little girl had been malnourished. Over the years, Tessa had donated small amounts to the home. It was what Cindy always requested in lieu of birthday and Christmas presents. It hit Tessa why supporting the home was so important. Immediately she felt guilty for her own self-pity. These kids had real problems. Problems that a move or new job could never fix.

"Who are you?" Sandy repeated.

"I'm Tessa." She smiled, pleased when Sandy smiled back. "A friend of Cindy's."

"Me, too," Sandy replied with utter sincerity.

A youngish woman swept into the room, holding a baby. Tessa guessed the little one was perhaps a year old. "Thanks for coming, Cindy. I'm sorry for the short notice." She smiled in Tessa's direction.

Cindy made the introductions. "Don't worry. We can't control accidents."

"My daughter took a tumble," Donna explained. "My husband's with her at the ER and it looks as though her arm is broken. And she's wanting Mommy."

"Of course," Tessa murmured. "I'm free today and can help."

"Oh, that's wonderful!" Donna exclaimed. "We have a lot of kids today, so all hands are appreciated."

"Donna's one of our best volunteers," Cindy said. "And we couldn't manage without her. Today she should have had backup."

Tessa realized that taking the day to spend with her had been a real sacrifice on Cindy's part. Shopping and tea didn't rate on the same scale as helping children. "Oh."

"Normally I could handle it. Just didn't expect a broken arm." Donna untied her apron. "I'll grab my purse and take off, then. I don't know how long I'll be."

"I do," Cindy replied. "We'll see you on your next volunteer day if that works. Your daughter needs you. Flynn has the kids and they're fine."

Tessa watched the exchange and an unexpected seed of determination sprouted. If these women could devote time to help the kids, she could, too.

Chapter Four

Tessa closed the book, finishing what must have been the dozenth one she'd read. In an instant another landed in her lap as a young boy handed her a Berenstain Bears book.

"Another?" she questioned, having already read two tales of the bears' exploits.

"Uh-huh." He nodded his head earnestly.

"Time to get to sleep," Cindy said over her shoulder. "Miss Tessa is spoiling you to pieces." There was fondness in her voice.

"I think word got out that I read more than one book each," Tessa admitted.

"I think you're right." Cindy laughed, not sounding a bit tired despite the hours she'd spent organizing, cooking, playing, reading, supervising and getting children ready for bed.

Pitching in, Tessa hadn't felt tired. Usually at the end of the day she was exhausted. The result of depression, she suspected. She'd done enough reading on the subject to recognize the symptoms. But today, tonight, reenergized, she felt she could easily go on for another eight hours. The young boy snuggled down after she read him another story.

The McNabs, the couple who lived at the house and worked full-time for the Children's Home, had returned from a weekend away. Most of the volunteers worked daytime hours. A few could be counted on for occasional night shifts but the bulk of that time was covered by the paid staff.

Tessa pulled the blanket up over the boy's arms. So sweet. He had been relentless during dinner, teasing the girls. Now, though, there was something about the peacefulness of a sleepy child... Swallowing, Tessa abruptly stood. Out of nowhere her breath caught, coming with difficulty. Everything was suddenly too much. Too close.

The boy's hand tugged hers. "Are you coming back tomorrow?"

Tessa tried to sound normal, not as though she felt pinched from the inside out. "I'm not sure."

Cindy apparently recognized her discomfort. "We can finish up. The McNabs have everything under control."

"Good." Tessa nodded. "Yes."

Cindy took her elbow, guiding her to the stairs. "It's been a long day."

Tessa swallowed, hating that the hurt was attacking in waves. She'd conquered it for hours. It had even seemed to go away. But now every poignant moment was an assault.

Blindly, she navigated the stairs. Cindy was close behind, grabbing their purses from the hall tree. She didn't really remember how, but she was in the car, Cindy driving.

"Would you like to stay over?" Cindy was asking. "Tomorrow we could have a nice breakfast before church."

Tessa shook her head, knowing instinctively that she needed to be alone.

"Okay, well, I'll take you home. But if you change your mind I can be over in a tick. It's no trouble."

Sanity returned. "You've been gone from your family all day. You really don't have to babysit me."

Cindy took her gaze from the road for a moment, staring. "That's not what I meant. It's just that you don't have to be alone. We're here for you."

"I know. And it's truly appreciated. But I need to be able to handle an evening alone."

"I shouldn't have thrown you into the middle of the kids," Cindy fretted.

"I volunteered," Tessa reminded her.

"Yes, but I know it's a tender subject. I wasn't thinking."

Seemed they were each determined to take the blame.

Tessa dug deep and found a tiny smile. "At least we're not blaming each other."

Cindy saw the smile and laughed. "I have days when I feel that I've jumped in the deep end before I learned to wade in the shallows." She turned, heading toward Morgan's home, which was close. "Will you promise me something?"

Tessa took a deep breath, still feeling the twitchy beat of her heart. "Depends on what it is."

"If you're lonely or just bored, call me. If you don't feel like coming over or having company, we can talk on the phone."

"I can't promise to do it every time," Tessa replied truthfully. Most days she felt she used up all her words during working hours and had few left for anything else. It was why her cupboards were relatively bare, her cottage virtually unchanged since she moved in. Talking required an energy that she couldn't seem to sustain. Her parents had commented on her sparse communications. Tonight's pain was subsiding, nearly extinguished. Suddenly exhausted, she rubbed her eyes. It seemed as if years had passed since her divorce.

"Okay," Cindy conceded. "I hope you'll feel like going to church tomorrow."

"I'll see."

Sensing Tessa's reluctance, Cindy was silent as she drove the short remaining distance.

Morgan's broad driveway was empty, all the cars enclosed in the garage, so it was difficult to determine just who was home. But it didn't matter. After saying goodbye to Cindy, all Tessa wanted to do was disappear into her cottage. Skirting the front of the house, she took the shortcut that led her past the rose arbor.

"You're home early for a Saturday night," Morgan spoke from the darkness.

Startled, she jumped.

"Sorry. Thought you saw me."

"No, I wasn't looking out into the yard." Tessa collected herself, gazing into the night, finally seeing that he sat on a curved stone bench. *What is he doing out in the dark alone?* Should she ask? Undecided, she hesitated.

"The smell of the roses," he explained, apparently sensing her curiosity. Morgan stood, moving into a patch of moonlight. "It's more distinct at night when it's still. The heat of the sun brings out the aroma and the cooler air seems to capture it."

It was a romantic notion, one she hadn't expected of him. "Oh."

"Did you have a good time?"

"A good time?" she echoed. "It wasn't exactly that kind of day. I was having tea with Cindy when she got called to the Children's Home. Wound up working there this afternoon...well, and this evening."

"What did you do there?" he questioned.

"Cooked, read stories. Stuff with the kids."

"Oh." He looked perplexed.

She wondered why. "Is that so amazing?"

"You don't have kids."

Tessa stiffened. "No, I don't."

He held up one hand. "It wasn't an accusation. Just seems like an unlikely way to spend a Saturday."

"Don't you want to spend Saturdays with Poppy?"

"I do as often as I can. Not as often as I want."

The day's ventures emboldened her. "Why not?"

"My job doesn't end at five o'clock on Friday. Pipelines leak, trucks break down. You know that."

Tessa still didn't understand why he insisted on such hands-on management. "Surely you can hire someone to help with your workload."

"Do you know how many small enterprises like mine are gobbled up every year? I have to make sure that doesn't happen to Harper. If I delegate away all the problem solving, I might not know if we're facing a major obstacle."

"Is it really that likely?" she questioned.

"Adair Petroleum built a large regional office here several years ago to handle their pipeline and trucking operations. The recession hit. Now one of the majors owns it. And most of the local people who worked at Adair found themselves out of jobs. I took on the ones I could, but I didn't have enough jobs to go around. If something happened to Harper, it would be devastating to this town. I won't let that happen on my watch."

"Oh."

"Yes. Rosewood thrives because we, the community, made a conscious decision to keep it alive, to keep out big business and superstores that shut down local mom-and-pop operations. The bed-and-breakfast has been in the same family for generations, the same for the café, bakery, drugstore, hardware… Well, you get the idea. This community takes care of its own. And I'm part of that—I have to be, with so many employees dependent on me. It's not easy, but if it's important it's worth the effort."

All admirable, Tessa realized. Still… "What about Poppy?"

He frowned. "What about her?"

"She seems a little lonely."

"Lonely?" he scoffed. "She has me, Dorothy, Alvin, my parents when they visit."

"It seems she's only around adults," Tessa said carefully, hoping not to anger him. "I mean she doesn't have playdates, the kind of thing other kids do."

"I didn't have playdates when I was growing up. My parents were growing the business. I turned out reasonably okay."

Tessa sensed she wasn't gaining any ground and was about to be told to mind her own business. "True." She hesitated, remembering Dorothy's comment about Morgan no longer attending church. "Does Poppy attend Sunday school?"

"No. Why?"

"Just thinking. There are other kids to interact with. They sing, hear stories, sometimes make an art project." Wincing, she gave in to another impulse. "I go every Sunday. She could come along with me."

"I don't know…"

Not sure of his religious convictions, she tried to be subtle. "Like I said, it's mostly a social thing.

I think Poppy would really like it. I see Cindy and Flynn there."

He seemed to waver. "What about the church session?"

"She could go to junior church," Tessa replied. "Lots of singing. Unless you have plans to do something with Poppy tomorrow."

"No. I have to meet with a pipeline supervisor, Ronnie Broussard. He's a key man in the field—East Texas. He's tied up all the time putting out figurative fires. We need this meeting."

She waited.

"I suppose it would be all right," he conceded, "for her to go with you tomorrow."

She wondered if the roses had softened him.

"But no preaching."

Or not.

"I don't want her to grow up with false promises," he continued, "and to believe everything's going to be all golden."

Tessa frowned, hating to think the child would be denied the joy of hope. "No?"

"Life has a way of squashing things. It's ridiculous to believe it can all be changed or fixed."

"It's not ridiculous," she replied quietly. "It's faith."

"It's pointless," he replied, bitterness infusing the words.

"You must have loved her a great deal."

Silence was sudden and thick.

"I don't need your amateur psychology or your meddling." He turned, his boots a distinctive thud on the stone walkway.

Morgan seemed to take the rose-scented air with him when he left. Too much emotion had been staked out on display today. She wasn't sure why she'd felt the need to prod him about Poppy, to question him about his late wife.

Following the puddles of moonlight, she made her way to the cottage. But, despite her best intentions, she turned around, watching as Morgan disappeared in the night.

It was plain to see Poppy was excited to wear her best dress and shoes by the way she eagerly smoothed the skirt. Her dress was blue, almost an exact match to her eyes, broken up with large white polka dots. Along with white tights and glossy white shoes, she was a picture. Her small fingers curled in Tessa's, sending a responding curl of warmth to her stomach. Such innocent trust in the gesture. If this little girl was hers, Tessa knew she would take walks with her just to capture her hand and hold it close.

"Are other kids gonna be there?" Poppy questioned again.

Tessa smiled, not minding the repetition. "Yes. Lots. You'll have a good time."

"Why didn't Daddy want to come?"

"He's busy with a special meeting."

"He always has work," Poppy replied.

Tessa squeezed the small hand. "But he misses you when he does," she improvised. Surely that was the case. "You're way more fun than work."

Poppy screwed her face into a puzzled frown. "You sure?"

"Very." Tessa led her small charge into the Sunday school building.

Rosewood Community Church had been constructed in the late 1800s. Weathering storms and even a fire, the faithful congregation kept the building well maintained. True to the Victorian age in which it was built, the lines of the church were classic. And, in Tessa's opinion, classy. She loved that the floors were constructed of local wood, original to the building. Designated on the historical register, the church conveyed its beautiful spirit visually, as well.

The fire that had erupted several years earlier hadn't stopped worship. Instead, they pulled together to rebuild. Members of other churches volunteered as well, offering materials, labor and donations. It was a church of the community and it had taken the whole community to repair the damage. But now the scars were scarce. Cindy told her they left one charred piece of timber, now enclosed in a case, to remind them of how fortunate they'd been not to lose the entire structure.

Once at her class, it didn't take long for Poppy to meet her Sunday school teacher, then greet the other children.

Tessa unobtrusively lingered in the hallway to make certain Poppy would be okay. But the child was all smiles, so Tessa finally made her way to her own class.

Her thoughts remained with Poppy. After Sunday school ended, she darted over to check on junior church, but again, Poppy was fine. Still, Tessa fidgeted during the church service. Usually she appreciated the beauty of the stained-glass windows, the aged wood, the flowers that adorned the altar. It was a place for her thoughts to settle, for her mind to seek solace. But today she glanced at her watch more than her Bible. And the moment the congregation dispersed, she practically ran to the chapel to collect Poppy.

Relieved to see that she was still looking happy, Tessa released a breath she hadn't realized she was holding. "So, you had a good time?"

"Uh-huh." Poppy waved a booklet. "And I have stories."

"That's great. If it's okay with your father, we can read them later."

"Can we come back again?"

"If your father agrees." All Tessa had previously gleaned was that Morgan wasn't a churchgoer. After last evening's conversation, it was evident why. She'd known others who had gone through crises of faith because of a loss. She considered herself fortunate to have held on tightly to her own despite Karl, despite the disappointment of knowing she would never bear children.

"Tomorrow?"

Tessa smiled. "Well, not tomorrow. It's called Sunday school because it meets on Sunday."

"But the party's on Saturday!" Poppy wailed.

Tessa noticed a sheet of bright orange paper stapled to the booklet. "Let's check out what your teacher sent."

Poppy was right. They were having a class skating party. She drew her eyebrows together. What would Morgan think of this? She had no idea. Which meant her best option was to distract Poppy so that she wouldn't worry over it right now. "I bet Dorothy will have lunch ready when we get home."

Shaking her head, Poppy lifted her gaze. "Sunday lunch is sandwiches. Daddy says Dorothy should have a day off."

Tessa had scrupulously kept to her own cottage on the weekends except when they were working on Saturdays, having asked Morgan to phone her if she was needed. But he hadn't called, so she didn't know how the house worked on Sundays. "That's nice. I love sandwiches. What about you?"

The small head lifted up, then down. "Uh-huh. Dorothy makes dessert on Saturday so we have good dessert for Sunday, too."

"Do you help?"

"Uh-huh," Poppy repeated.

Driving back to Morgan's house, Tessa wondered

when he would return. She would have to speak with him about Saturday's party. Tessa might have successfully distracted the little girl for the time being, but it wasn't likely that Poppy would forget about the party entirely.

Sure enough, as soon as Poppy spotted Dorothy, she rushed to show her the papers she'd brought home. Dorothy met Tessa's gaze. She could see her own question in the other woman's eyes.

"Can I have chips?" Poppy was asking Dorothy.

"Yes. But before lunch, let's change out of your good dress."

Poppy swirled, the full skirt responding to the pirouette, swishing prettily. "Okay. Can I wear my purple shirt?"

Dorothy concurred as they headed up the back stairs.

Tessa released her breath. She knew she was overly invested in the outcome of whether Poppy would be allowed to attend the party. She wondered how wise it had been to have pushed for Poppy to attend church.

Morgan was nowhere in sight. But she could imagine his expression when he learned about Saturday's party. Last night he'd been downright grim at the prospect of Poppy attending church. She hated to imagine his reaction when he heard about a second outing.

Chapter Five

Morgan flexed his shoulders, but the knot between them didn't dissipate. Weariness settled in his bones as he walked from the garage to the house. His *quick* meeting had turned into a marathon. New problems cropped up like dandelions in the spring.

Landowners weren't happy about the cleanup from a recent pipeline leak in East Texas. Ronnie Broussard had consulted with him, followed procedure, but one owner had made a career of keeping his neighbors riled up. Not that Morgan expected people to be happy about oil spills. But Harper's cleanup record was the quickest and most efficient for any size transporter. It was something he took pride in.

The dull ache beneath his eyebrows that never seemed to go away intensified. He didn't want to believe the constant headaches interfered with his judgment, but on long days like this one he wondered. Had he done all he should on this last leak? Or had details become blurred? He couldn't put the blame on anyone else. Ronnie had followed orders. Just as Tessa had.

She had surprised him with her utter efficiency and dedication to the job. He had expected a steeper learning curve, but her experience and expertise had eliminated the need. Instead, she had made certain that he knew about the leak immediately, then made the calls necessary for a complete and thorough spill cleanup.

If she had been at the helm during the Exxon Valdez spill, history would have been rewritten. Fortunately, Harper's spills weren't on that scale. He spent plenty on maintenance and bought the best steel pipe on the market for replacements. It wasn't a popular choice these days. A lot of his competitors bought the cheapest steel possible. But he refused to endanger the environment. Poppy had to grow up in this world, and he wanted to make sure he did his part to maintain the land under his control.

Morgan remembered all the people who advised him to take the company public, leave these decisions to someone else. He shifted the computer tablet in his hand. That step wasn't something he was prepared to do.

Still, the exhaustion weighed on him. The previous day had been twenty-two continuous hours. And today's meeting had begun early, then lasted late. He had expected to be home around three o'clock, not eight in the evening.

Knowing the back door was unlocked, he pocketed his keys. Pushing the door open, he was surprised by the hum of voices. It was time for Poppy to be in bed. Searching the room, he spotted his daughter, decked out in her favorite jammies, sitting at the table. And for some reason Tessa sat with her.

Dorothy noticed him first. "Well, it's about time."

He smiled at her despite his fatigue. He knew she worried about him like a parent. "Took longer than I expected."

"Now, that's what I'd call an understatement," she replied, smoothing the sides of her cross-stitched apron in place.

"What's going on?" He caught Poppy, who had climbed down from her chair and launched herself at him.

"Tessa made special cocoa," Poppy told him, her small arms encircling his neck.

"Oh?"

Tessa fidgeted. "Just a brand I especially like. My mother sent a care package."

"She afraid you've landed in the boonies?"

Looking mortified, Tessa shook her head. "No, of course not. She just spoils me. Looks like I'm doing the same thing."

"I told her we often have cocoa in the evening," Dorothy added with a look that dared him to counter her words.

"Would you like some?" Tessa questioned. "You must be hungry."

"Yes, you must," Dorothy chimed in. "We had

leftover stew for dinner. Guessed you might be late so I made sure to cook something that warms up even better than the original."

How could he argue with someone as caring as Dorothy? He wasn't hungry, but common sense told him he should eat. "Sounds good, Dorothy. Thanks."

"It has baby carrots and baby peas," Poppy told him. "And it's really good."

"Everything Dorothy cooks is really good," he agreed, putting his tablet on the counter, glancing at the screen before he turned it off.

Tessa lit the burner beneath a pan of milk. "Won't take a moment to fix another cup of cocoa."

He started to protest, but the wall of goodwill was overpowering. And he didn't have the energy to surmount it. Dorothy scooped some stew into a bowl. Once in the microwave, the warming dinner emitted aromas reserved for waking the deadest of appetites.

Only a few minutes later, Tessa set a mug of hot cocoa in front of him. "I hope you'll like it."

He nodded. It was something he'd usually skip, but he didn't want to be rude.

"Taste it, Daddy. It's real good."

He took an obligatory sip. Surprised, he glanced up. "This really is good."

"It's bittersweet," Tessa explained. "Most hot cocoa is milk chocolate, a little sweet for me."

"She put lots of marshmallows in mine," Poppy explained, adding a cocoa mustache to her face with another sip. "So it would be sweeter."

"You're pretty sweet already," he told his darling girl.

She grinned. "You always think that."

Yes, yes, he did.

Dorothy placed a heaping bowl of stew in front of him. "I know you didn't get your three squares today."

He'd taken off before breakfast. There was a vague memory of a few doughnuts and coffee. Endless cups of coffee. And he'd skipped lunch.

"I ate my stew at dinner," Poppy informed him.

"It is good," Tessa chimed in.

Dorothy looked down at him, then raised her eyebrows.

Picking up a spoon, he dug in, knowing it wouldn't be wise to say he was too tired to eat. He swallowed a bite. "Delicious."

Glancing up, he caught Tessa's concerned stare. She met his eyes, then finally looked down. What was in her aquamarine gaze?

"I'm going to a party!" Poppy announced.

"Party?" He looked at his daughter. "What party?"

"At sunny school," Poppy replied.

That had been today, he realized. But he hadn't intended for it to be an ongoing thing. When Tessa brought up the subject, it had seemed harmless, a onetime outing. "What's she talking about?"

Tessa cleared her throat. "The teacher gave her a handout. The younger grades are having a little party on Saturday. Should be fun with lots of kids."

He frowned. "I didn't sign on for a series of church events."

Poppy's lower lip began to quiver. "I wanna go, Daddy."

His throat tightened. There was little in the world he could deny her. "I have to think about it."

"It's time for bed," Dorothy said only a moment later, preempting tears and hurt feelings. "Freckles looks sleepy."

Temporarily distracted, Poppy clutched Freckles, her favorite stuffed pal. "We're not sleepy."

"Oh, I think we will be," Dorothy rebutted.

Still reluctant, Poppy slipped off her chair and clasped Dorothy's outstretched hand.

Silence prevailed in the kitchen as the duo left, until Morgan and Tessa heard their footsteps recede.

"You've stirred up a hornet's nest," Morgan began.

"What?" At odds with the response, her eyes filled with dismay. "I mean, I don't believe so."

"Your reply shows you know exactly what I mean." He pushed the mostly uneaten stew aside. "You've put me in an untenable situation. If I agree, then I'm encouraging more church participation. If I refuse, I'm the bad guy."

"It's just a skating party," she reasoned. "It's not a church service. And she had such a good time today with the other children. She needs that in her life."

"You've become an expert on Poppy pretty fast." Provoked, Morgan tried to bank his temper, but his fierce protective instincts resisted. "I should never have agreed to let her go to church."

"Then why did you?"

Because he'd been distracted, busy, too caught up in his thoughts about work to give it much thought. When Tessa had asked him, he'd tried to wave her away, instead agreeing so she would leave him alone. But that wasn't something he wanted to admit. "You said it was a good social outing for Poppy."

"It was," she agreed.

"But I never said going to church would be a regular practice."

"No," she agreed. "You didn't. This is a party." Her eyebrows lifted as though underscoring the meaning of the word.

Morgan sighed. How did he refuse his daughter a party? His head lapsed back a fraction, leaning against the tallest rung of the chair as his weariness deepened. At times he felt as though one more decision would break him. Brittle as the caged pain, he felt he could fracture into a million pieces. But that was the easy way out. "You're treading a fine line."

Tessa lifted her chin. "Is my job on that line?"

He wasn't going to refute her question. Because it was. Anyone who threatened Poppy's best interests would be gone in a moment. His daughter was the most important thing in the world to him. Period.

"I see." Tessa pushed back her dark hair, left loose, unlike the tight upsweep she adopted while working. She looked younger, Morgan realized. Her features seemed softer somehow. Without the suit, the severe hairstyle, the camouflage, she also seemed more vulnerable.

"Please think about the party," she added when he didn't speak. "Think about what it would mean to Poppy."

"You might want to consider what you're saying," he advised, needing her to stop pushing.

Tessa shrugged. "I don't have that much left to lose."

Her words were so quiet he wondered for a moment if he'd imagined them. The thought barely took form before she turned and left, the kitchen door closing behind her.

The following morning Tessa waited for the call, expected the call to tell her she no longer had a job. She drank two extra cups of coffee. Still no word. So she put her hair up and her suit on. The walk from her cottage to the house seemed interminably long.

Quiet. It came from both the main level and upstairs. Unlike in newer homes, the sound didn't travel from the upper level unless it was extremely loud. But she didn't hear the patter of Dorothy in the kitchen, either. Or Alvin. Of course, he could be outside. Where was Poppy?

Could they all still be asleep? Checking her watch, Tessa tapped it, then walked to the grandfather clock in the foyer. No, it was definitely past eight o'clock. By this time, Morgan normally had been at work for hours. The study was empty but he could be at the main office, at the tank farm, out in the field. That, however, didn't explain the absence of everyone else.

She looked at Morgan's computer, turned off. There wasn't a message on her desk, the calls weren't forwarded. As she walked back into the foyer, her footsteps echoed, punctuated by the occasional creaking of the heart of pine floor.

The stillness couldn't be because of her. Even though she had considered packing her belongings the previous night, leaving before being fired, she knew the family wouldn't all desert the house because of her.

Tessa felt an unexpected chill as the emptiness stared back at her. Clutching her elbows, she rubbed the skin on her arms to chase away the goose bumps.

A telephone shrilled and she jumped. "Quit being so melodramatic," she scolded herself. "It's a telephone, perfectly normal." Still, she scurried to the phone situated on a cherry table near the stairway landing. "Hello?"

"Any word on Dorothy?" a woman asked.

"Word?" Tessa echoed.

"This is Janet Divo from Harper's main office. I tried calling Morgan's cell but it went straight to voice mail."

"Oh." Tessa was at a loss.

"Um. Who is this?" Janet asked.

"Tessa Pierce. I'm—"

"I know who you are. Well, good to *meet* you. Do you have any news on Dorothy?"

Could this get any more awkward? Tessa cleared her throat. "I don't know what's going on."

"Oh."

The awkwardness quadrupled.

"So what is it?" Tessa asked.

Janet paused. "I'm sorry to tell you that Dorothy's had a stroke. At least that was the initial thought. Morgan's message was brief."

"So they're all at the hospital?"

Janet muttered something under her breath. "Are you the only one there?"

Needlessly, Tessa spun slowly in a circle. "I'm afraid so."

"The message was left around five-thirty this morning," Janet continued.

"I'm guessing there's only one hospital."

Tessa had the impression Janet was nodding.

"Um, yes, I'm sorry," Janet vocalized. "Just wondering if you'd mind calling me when you do know something."

"Sure." Tessa pulled open the small drawer fronting the table, finding a pad and pen. "Let me get your direct number. And can you give me directions to the hospital?"

Information in hand, Tessa retrieved her purse from the cottage and climbed into her car. A stroke? Dorothy looked perfectly fine the day before. She frowned. Well, not exactly. She'd been worried about

Morgan's reaction to the party, Poppy's possible disappointment. Swallowing, Tessa wondered if the worry could have caused high blood pressure or whatever had triggered the stroke.

Like most everything in Rosewood, the hospital was only minutes away and easy to find. It was a modern facility, large enough that she guessed it was fully equipped.

The woman at the front desk confirmed that Dorothy wasn't yet in a room. Maybe her condition wasn't as bad as Tessa had expected. Encouraged, she located the emergency room. Morgan and Poppy sat in the relatively small waiting area. She assumed Alvin was with Dorothy.

Poppy spotted her and jumped up. Morgan watched, catching sight of Tessa, then standing, as well.

"Janet Divo phoned to check on the situation— she told me where to find you," Tessa began. "How is Dorothy?"

Poppy's small face crumpled. "She's all sick."

Morgan shot Tessa a disbelieving look as he picked up his daughter.

Realizing that she was making matters worse, Tessa impulsively stroked the child's arm. "But she's here with all the wonderful doctors and nurses who can make her all better."

Poppy looked up at her father. "Really?"

Indecision warred in his expression. It suddenly struck Tessa how painful this must be for him. Having lost his wife suddenly, now finding himself back in the emergency room, the experience must have brought back terrible memories.

Tessa didn't care if it cost her job. "Doctors and nurses care very much about people who get sick and they work very hard to make them better. Tell me, what did you eat for breakfast?"

"I grabbed some crackers out of a vending machine for her," Morgan admitted.

"Well, I bet we can find the cafeteria." She met his gaze, trying to convey that she would keep Poppy safe while he checked on Dorothy. "Can we bring you back anything?"

He shook his head.

Guessing he hadn't eaten much in more than twenty-four hours, Tessa decided to bring back something for him. She found a bagel with ham and cream cheese as well as some orange juice. There was a coffeemaker in the ER waiting room, but she guessed he could use something with a vitamin or two.

Poppy ate scrambled eggs, bacon and a piece of toast. Finishing a small carton of milk, she looked better than she had only twenty minutes earlier.

"Are you sure they can fix Dorothy?"

Tessa knew how wrong it was to make a child a promise that might not be kept. "I'm sure they will try their very best."

"Daddy had to carry her out to the car," Poppy confided in a quiet voice. "And Alvin looked all scared."

He was probably terrified. The couple had spent their entire adult lives together. Tessa still held hope that Dorothy wasn't in a bad condition. It worried her that the older woman remained in the emergency room. Maybe there was a shortage of beds in the regular rooms. That could explain why she was still in the ER.

While Poppy sipped her milk, Tessa pulled out her phone, texting Cindy the bare facts. She didn't want Poppy to hear her asking Morgan about Dorothy. Because of privacy laws, the staff wouldn't tell her anything. Dorothy's condition might not be serious, but it was frightening for a young child.

Cindy replied within a few minutes, saying she would contact someone she knew at the hospital to find out more.

Morgan was still in the waiting room when they returned. Although he accepted the food she offered, he put the bagel sandwich and juice on a side table next to the magazines.

"You really need to eat something," Tessa told him quietly.

His gaze didn't leave the treatment area door. "In a while."

And Tessa couldn't find it in herself to lecture. Too many people had lectured her about eating in recent months. "Would you like some more coffee?"

Morgan shrugged. Deciding the motion wasn't a rebuff, Tessa poured coffee into two disposable cups, adding a small bit of sugar to his. She handed it to him when she heard the quiet dinging of her cell phone. It was a text from Cindy. Call me when you're alone and can talk.

With Poppy parked beside her father, Tessa eased away from the waiting room. It took only a few minutes to find some privacy and phone Cindy.

"Were you able to reach your friend?" Tessa asked, referring to one of Cindy's many contacts.

"Yes." Cindy paused. "It's not good."

Tessa's hopes fell. "Is it a stroke?"

"Yes," Cindy confirmed. "And a bad one. They're admitting her to the primary care unit, which is just a teeny step below ICU."

Tessa's breath caught.

"She's looking at a long recovery," Cindy continued.

"But she will recover?"

"Tessa, it's going to be rough. It's possible she may not recover completely."

Tessa thought of her grandmother's mild stroke, how within weeks she seemed to be back to normal. "But surely—"

"Morgan doesn't need false hope."

"This doesn't sound like you, Cindy."

"I'll be praying for Dorothy, but we have to be realistic. It almost killed Morgan when he lost Lucy. Dorothy's always been like a second mother to him. I want her to get well! But I don't want Morgan to be encouraged that she'll be fine if…if things don't work out that way."

Tessa clutched her phone. "He and Poppy have already lost too much. Are you sure the doctor is good?"

"The best." Cindy paused. "I wonder if Morgan will call his parents back as reinforcements."

"Back?"

"They put off their retirement plans when Lucy died."

"What sort of plans?" Tessa asked.

"Travel. When his father headed the business, there was never enough time for real vacations."

Tessa instantly pictured an older version of Morgan, finally unburdened. Before she could change her mind, she spoke. "That won't be necessary. I can help until...until Dorothy's better."

Cindy made a strangled noise.

Tessa ignored it. "And, yes, I realize now that might be some time. But it's not as though I have a busy social life. I can help watch Poppy. I have a lot of—" she swallowed "—empty hours."

"That will be a comfort to Morgan," Cindy replied after a pause. "But what about you? You're still fragile yourself."

"Not in the same way." Tessa thought of her hours of self-examination. And self-pity. Seemed terribly selfish now. "I'm not sure what I lost was ever worth keeping."

There was silence.

So Tessa rushed on, "I've got to get back to the emergency room. If they have Dorothy's room ready,

Morgan will want to go up and see her. I'll need to watch Poppy."

"Tessa?" Cindy questioned. "Please, be careful. I care about you, too."

"You have the biggest heart in the state," she murmured. "I'll be careful."

Retracing her steps, Tessa saw that Morgan hadn't moved since she left. "Any word?"

He turned. "They're going to move her to PCU."

She nodded, knowing from Cindy what that meant. "As soon as she can have visitors, I can watch Poppy while you check on her."

Morgan's gaze flickered. "You don't have to."

"I want to." Impulsively, she laid one hand over his. "Please. I need to."

Confusion and gratitude swam in his dark eyes. Then he glanced down at her hand.

Mortified, she pulled it back, sticking both hands behind her back. "If you don't mind, I'll walk with Poppy to the gift shop—get her a treat for being so well behaved and patient."

He glanced up at the doorway leading into the emergency room. "Fine."

She had seen the gift shop in the front of the hospital when she first came in. It was small, but it would be a diversion.

Poppy looked at her father for permission, then slipped her hand into Tessa's. So much trust in the small gesture. No wonder Morgan was protective.

Looking past the display of candies and chips,

Tessa spotted what she'd hoped for. A coloring book and crayons. Low-tech. But she knew Poppy loved to color. She let the child choose some gum. The treat was something new for Poppy. Dorothy had explained that they'd just introduced gum about a month earlier when they could be sure she wouldn't swallow it.

Poppy picked up a chocolate bar. "Can we get this for Daddy?"

Tessa felt a lump forming in her throat at the youngster's consideration. "Sure."

Having paid, they walked slowly back to the waiting room. Morgan remained in the same position, concentrating on the treatment doorway.

Tessa could tell that he wished he could see inside, to make certain Dorothy was being cared for. But the look on his face...it was sheer agony. The thought flashed like an electrified sign. If she guessed correctly, he was reliving the loss of his wife while worrying about another woman who had been in his life since it had begun.

Gently she stroked Poppy's hair and wondered if she really would be able to shoulder the emotions now spilling like an unleashed silo of grain.

Chapter Six

Morgan cautiously entered the hospital room. He had waited. And waited. Alvin remained at Dorothy's side, his ashen face streaked with tears. Nurses and aides continued their parade in and out of the room. Morgan had intended to wait until they all finished. Finally a nurse told him there wouldn't be a solitary moment, to go ahead in.

Swallowing, Morgan braced himself, then looked at Dorothy. Pale, she'd never looked so pale. And one side of her face sagged downward. Eyes closed, she was so still she looked as though she'd stopped breathing. But the slew of machines hooked up to her beeped and gurgled in precision. A digital readout showed her heart rate, blood pressure and oxygen level.

He couldn't imagine his life without Dorothy in it. Any more than he could without his parents. She and Alvin had begun working for his parents about ten years before he was born. Dorothy had been an indulgent second mother. Extra treats, extra love.

When he was very young she told him he was much like a little boy she had loved. But she'd never told him who that boy was. Years later his father had explained that Alvin and Dorothy had one child, a boy who'd died when he was just four years old. That was the year before Morgan had been born.

He literally had known Dorothy forever.

She had always been so strong. Capable, wise, insightful. But most of all, strong. Now she looked devastatingly weak. Briefly he lifted his gaze upward, wanting to ask for help, knowing how futile it would be.

Alvin spotted him. "Morgan."

Quietly, Morgan approached the bedside. "You holding up?"

Alvin nodded, but Morgan could see that it was barely a truth. Usually a rock, Alvin seemed to have shrunk. The hand holding Dorothy's was shaking.

Knowing exactly how his friend was feeling, Morgan swallowed. "Alvin, you know I've stood in your shoes."

Seconds ticked by. Alvin finally nodded.

"But there's hope for Dorothy. The doctors said we got her here so fast that much of the worst damage was avoided." *At least they hope so.*

"Yeah." But there was no conviction in his voice.

"I'd be worried, too," Morgan told him truthfully. "But that's our job. Speaking of which, I don't want you to give one thought to the house. I'll get someone from town to fill in as long as it takes. For you and Dorothy."

Alvin looked back at his wife. "She was going to make cookies today with Poppy."

"She'll do that when she's well."

Gripping Dorothy's hand more firmly, Alvin hung on as though she was his lifeline.

Because she was, Morgan knew.

"You'll want to be with her, so I'll pack a change of clothes, things you'll need, and bring it back later," Morgan told him. "And I'll spell you when you're ready."

"No." Alvin shook his head. "I need to be here."

Which would be exhausting. Still, Morgan didn't doubt Alvin would carry through. But he was at an age that would make the marathon watch difficult.

Morgan resolved to spell Alvin. His thoughts skidded to a halt. He'd always had Dorothy and Alvin to watch Poppy, in fact to help raise Poppy. How was he going to be any help to his friends while caring for his daughter all on his own? Possibilities flirted in his mind. Maybe he could call Cindy, see if she could pinch-hit a few times while he came to the hospital.

Leaving Dorothy's room, Morgan stopped at the unit's nursing desk and provided his phone numbers. Realizing Tessa was still in the waiting room with Poppy, he upped his stride. The elevator seemed to creep as it descended. He rushed through the corridors, hoping Tessa wasn't completely overwhelmed.

Giggles punctuated the air as he approached the

waiting room. Familiar giggles. And there was his daughter, chattering away with Tessa as she…no, *they* colored.

"Daddy!" Poppy jumped up from her chair. "Can I go see Dorothy now?"

Morgan lifted her in his arms. "Not right now. Dorothy's sleeping."

Poppy furrowed her tiny brow. "But it's daytime."

Morgan paused.

So Tessa spoke. "You take naps."

"But Dorothy doesn't," Poppy objected.

"Sometimes grown-ups need naps, too. Do you know that it's when we're sleeping that we get well when we need to?"

"Really?"

"Really." Tessa made a swiping motion across her chest. "Cross my heart."

Poppy looked up at Morgan. "Really?"

He nodded, his throat tight as he set her down.

"I got you a treat," Poppy told him, changing the subject without blinking. She turned around and re-trieved the chocolate bar. "Like Dorothy does for us."

"I hope it's all right," Tessa began. "She picked out gum for herself."

"Yes, fine." He wondered why she and Poppy had been laughing, but didn't want to question Tessa when she had gone the extra mile to entertain Poppy. Instead, he tried to take stock of the day. "We can forward the calls to the main office."

"Done. I spoke to Janet while I was at the house. She forwarded the calls remotely."

That was a relief. "Good," he murmured. "I need to get some things together for Alvin."

"Poppy and I can hang out," Tessa offered.

Morgan frowned. "I was going to call Cindy."

"She's offered her help, but I think I can handle it."

He looked at her in question, wondering how Cindy could possibly know about Dorothy already.

"I also called Cindy," Tessa explained, picking up the coloring book and crayons. "I'd take Poppy with me now, but I don't have a car seat for her."

"She just graduated to a booster seat instead of a traditional car seat," he replied inanely, his mind still in the room upstairs where Dorothy was lying so still. "I'll head home now. Have a lot to take care of."

"Can I help?" Tessa asked.

Morgan shook his head. "No, takes Rosewood insider info. I need someone to temporarily clean and cook, and also someone to keep up the grounds. Janet should be able to find someone."

But a day later, Morgan learned that it wasn't going to be that easy. Clicking off his phone, he slammed it on the desktop harder than he intended.

"I don't know if I should ask," Tessa began as she stepped out of her office that was aligned with his, "but was that about Dorothy?"

"Not directly. Janet gave me some prospects to work here in the house. I can hire a woman who cooks but doesn't clean, or one who cleans but doesn't cook."

Tessa stepped closer. "Have you considered hiring them both?"

His eyes widened.

"Just keeping the house clean is a full-time job. There aren't that many housekeepers these days, ones who take on full responsibility for the house, the meals, everything."

"You're right, I suppose. When Dorothy began working here, it was a different time." He rubbed his forehead, willing the pain to leave. "In reality a different century."

"I can help with some of Dorothy's more…personal duties," Tessa offered.

"Such as?"

"Just the little things involved in running a house. Keeping up with the mail, grocery shopping, getting Poppy up and dressed, then back down in the evenings, that sort of thing."

"I'm sure one of the women will be able to watch Poppy." Lifting his gaze, he wondered why Tessa suddenly paled.

"Whatever you think is best. Did you find a man for the outside tasks?"

"I'm working on it." His thoughts switched tracks. "I'll need the Lawson contract as soon as you can finish it."

Tessa nodded, then returned through the arched opening to her own office.

* * *

Tessa watched Poppy, who was busy setting up a tea party for Freckles and friends. It had seemed natural, bringing toys in from the family room to her office. Poppy had claimed one corner behind the desk, leaving plenty of room for Tessa.

Working on the contract, it was easy to glance at Poppy and make certain she was all right. Since Poppy had been coming into her office from the first day, it seemed pretty natural having her playing close by.

Poppy tugged on her arm, offering one of her tiny teacups.

"Oh, my favorite!" Tessa exclaimed, accepting the empty cup filled with pretend tea.

"Milk?"

"Please."

Poppy picked up the small beaker and poured in a swig of pretend milk.

Tessa stirred her cup.

"Sugar?" Poppy questioned seriously.

"Yes, please. One spoonful."

Again Poppy was very careful with the pretend sugar.

Once completed, Tessa mock sipped at the tea. "Yummy."

Poppy smiled. Her simple joy caused a twinge of regret. Tessa was relishing this time with the child, but when Morgan hired the women to care for the house, Poppy wouldn't be spending her days close by. She wondered if the women would be able to take the little girl to playdates, parties and the Rainbow class. Things she had hoped Morgan would agree to. Glancing at her calendar, she realized the skating party was coming up. Would Morgan mellow on the issue?

By tacit agreement, pizza was on the dinner menu. They had very little food delivery service in their small town.

Even though she had also ordered salads and put out a veggie tray and fruit, Tessa silently hoped Morgan would hire a cook soon. She had volunteered, but he'd insisted that she needed to work on the monthly reports. And she couldn't really argue with that. Unfortunately, Dorothy's stroke coincided with one of the busiest times for Tessa's duties.

But she'd had time to prepare a simple lunch for Poppy, then coax her into a nap. Morgan conducted business by phone, not seeming to notice that for every leak in the dam she plugged, another one popped open. She remembered Morgan telling her that she could call on Janet if she needed extra help.

Frowning, she also remembered Morgan's assurance that one of the women he hired would be taking care of Poppy. No point in bothering Janet if that was the case.

But for tonight she could bathe Poppy, get her ready for bed and imagine what it would be like to care for this little one always.

* * *

A day later Morgan didn't feel like slamming the phone. Instead he let his face sag into his hands. What was the world coming to? He had hired both a cook, Nancy, and a cleaner, Heather. But he was floored when both stated outright that they wouldn't watch Poppy. That, each explained, was a job unto itself.

Was Dorothy in fact a superhero? Disguised as a housekeeper of mature years?

And where was he going find a nanny/babysitter?

"Here," Tessa said from her adjoining office.

His head jerked up. Had he been speaking aloud?

"Right where you left it, Poppy." Tessa laughed. "Or do you think Freckles ran in here by himself?"

Poppy giggled. "He might've."

"Oh, you." Tessa gave Poppy a casual hug. "How about picking up the blocks? Once they're in the box, you can get out your paints." She walked back toward her desk, out of his line of vision.

Morgan sank back in his chair. Tessa had offered to watch Poppy, but that option came with too many complications, he decided. He clicked through the contact list on his phone and called Cindy. She should know someone.

"Thanks anyway." He ended the conversation in a near sigh within just a few minutes. "Yes, let me know if you hear of anyone. Okay." He clicked off the phone. Cindy had told him that he could probably find someone who would sit for Poppy, but not in his home. She had explained that the available women most likely had children of their own and would watch Poppy only in their own homes. The knot in his gut told him that wasn't going to happen.

He thought of his parents. If he asked…he knew they would return and care for Poppy. Was that fair?

A second knot in his stomach gave him his answer.

So what? What was he going to do?

"Morgan?" Tessa's voice jarred him. "Sorry to bother you, but I need the casing head figures."

"Sure." He swung his chair toward the computer, quickly vaulting between worlds. And therein lay the thorn. He was needed in both worlds. The business wasn't just his livelihood. Jobs for far too many people depended on its success.

But Poppy was the most important person in the world to him. He couldn't shortchange her. It seemed no matter which direction he chose, he'd be shortchanging someone. His daughter, his employees, his parents.

Automatically, he pulled up the information Tessa needed. Funny how she could work and keep an eye on Poppy. Seemed to come naturally.

He emailed her the casing head figures, automatically pulling up the ones on condensate as well, putting them in a separate email.

Then, not wanting to, he opened the file on nannies that he had begun not long after Poppy was born. Résumé after résumé. Not one he scanned gave him a sense of reassurance. They were dated, four years old now, he remembered. And that had been such a rough time. He had barely been able to breathe. He certainly hadn't been able to analyze résumés.

Picking up the phone, he called the agency that had supplied the candidates. They weren't local, but the closest to Rosewood. He was able to specify that he expected the right nanny to relocate. As Tessa had done. That hadn't been difficult. He took a deep breath and cleared his head. By this time next week, the new nanny should be installed and his house back to normal.

Chapter Seven

Saturday dawned fresh and sweet, filled with that unique smell of grass moist with an overnight blush of dew. Somewhere, from deeper in the country and far-off fields, horses neighed and cows munched fresh hay.

Tessa could also smell muffins baking. Blueberry if she wasn't mistaken. Nancy had proved to be a good cook, but they all missed Dorothy. The temporary loss of their friend and house manager seemed keenest when they gathered for a meal. Dorothy's and Alvin's chairs remained empty, the kitchen felt hollow, unloved. Their routines had changed dramatically, as well. Tessa was now at the house seven days a week, barely escaping long enough to sleep.

After pouring a cup of coffee from the pot on the sideboard, she reached for the creamer. The rest of the breakfast fare sat in serving bowls lined in a precise row beside the coffee. Serving breakfast in this style was Nancy's way of doing things. There wasn't anything wrong with it, just not as cozy as Dorothy's methods.

Hoping Morgan had risen on the sunny side of his bed, she picked up a piece of toast. She hadn't braved asking him if he'd rethought allowing Poppy to attend the skating party. Bringing up the subject seemed completely inappropriate with all that he was struggling to manage. But she guessed Dorothy would want the best for Poppy.

"Just toast?" Morgan questioned, coming up behind her, then skirting the table to stand in front of the sideboard.

She nodded. "For now. Poppy awake?"

"Yep. Says she has a big day, whatever that means."

Tessa cleared her throat.

Morgan slowly turned around. "You know what the big day is about?"

"Yes." His gaze was unnerving and she squirmed. "That is, I think so."

"Want to share your thoughts?"

Her palms began to sweat. "With everything that's been going on, Dorothy and all…"

His expression told her to hurry and say what she had to say.

"Anyway, this afternoon is the party."

He stared at her blankly. "What party?"

"The skating party."

"For Poppy?"

"Well, it's not for just Poppy," she explained. "But, yes, she's invited and it's this afternoon."

"I don't have time for—"

"I can take her," Tessa interrupted before he could fully refuse. "Wouldn't be any trouble. I bought a booster seat for my car." Swallowing, she paused for a few moments. "If it's all right with you."

"Maybe it'll take her mind off Dorothy," he said, surprising Tessa. "She's been begging to go see her."

Tessa nodded.

"So you know that, too?"

"It's been the theme of the week."

"Right." He added some sugar to his coffee. Then he picked up a plate, choosing eggs and ham. He sat in his usual chair at the head of the table, putting him next to Tessa.

She nervously tried to break the silence. "I believe I smelled muffins baking."

"Why don't you get one?" he asked.

Tessa shrugged. "I don't really want one. Just thought you might."

"Let me guess—until Dorothy's better you're going to nag me to eat, et cetera?"

She blinked. It wasn't a role she envisioned for herself. "Is that how I come across?"

For a moment he looked nonplused. "No, of course not. Just strange here without Dorothy." He took uncommon care cutting his ham. It was as though he didn't want to make eye contact.

Tessa fiddled with her cup.

Morgan noticed the motion, so she stilled her rest-less fingers. Was she so starched and predictable that she came across as a nag? Was that how Karl had viewed her? Was it more than the issue of children that had chased him away?

Morgan needed to make sure that Poppy was all right. Feeling unsettled, he had to get things under control. After agreeing to the party, he belatedly remembered why he'd initially quashed the idea. He didn't have anything against the people who at-tended Rosewood Community Church. It was the false promise he didn't want his daughter buying into.

Glancing at his watch, he saw that it was past time for the party to start. He swung into the park-ing lot at the skating rink. Not too many rinks left, he'd heard. Guess skating wasn't all that cool any-more.

He paid the admission and adjusted his eyes to the flashing lights in the rink. Not sure who would be in the group other than Poppy and Tessa, he re-alized he hadn't asked for details. Not like him. But his thoughts had been consumed with worry about Dorothy. Over the week she had shown a tiny bit of improvement, but was facing a long uphill fight.

There seemed to be dozens of kids zooming around the wood-floored rink. Some parents held toddlers' hands, others trailed behind speeding teen-agers who wore inline skates. It occurred to him that he'd never taken Poppy skating. Blinking, he wondered why. Business seemed to fill every hour, but still…

Then he spotted them. Tessa caught his attention, her dark hair loose and long, framing her heart-shaped face. Relaxed and smiling, she looked like a different woman from the one who worked for him. It wasn't just the casual clothes. It was her entire posture.

Morgan guessed that if he could see her unusual eyes, they would be sparkling.

Tessa held Poppy's hand, then reached out with the other, carefully steering them into a gentle circle. The rotation put him in her line of vision.

He could tell the instant she saw him. Her posture stiffened, her arms suddenly rigid. Leaning down, she spoke to Poppy.

Seeing him, his daughter waved happily. "Daddy!"

Morgan walked to the railing, meeting them halfway. "Having fun?"

Her head moved up and down eagerly. "Tessa said we could buy skates for me."

Tessa cleared her throat. "Actually, I said we'd ask your dad what he thought of you having your own pair." She lifted her gaze. "To skate at home," she explained. "I used to love mine as a kid."

"Where are your skates?" Poppy asked him.

"I don't need skates."

"They won't let you out on the floor without 'em," she told him seriously.

"I don't need to be out on the floor."

Poppy instantly looked crushed. "How come?"

"Well, you and Tessa are doing fine."

"Don't you *want* to skate with me?" Poppy questioned, her bottom lip beginning to quiver.

"That's not the point," he protested.

Tessa's eyebrows lifted, signaling it *was* the point.

"Well, I don't have skates," he reasoned.

Poppy stuck out her foot. "Tessa rented 'em. You could, too."

Tessa glanced downward, but not before he glimpsed a flicker of amusement. He needed to get back to his work. Glancing at his watch, he saw that his phone conference was only an hour away. Looking back at Poppy, he saw the hope in her eyes, realizing he couldn't disappoint her. "Just for a little while."

She clapped her small hands together.

Once he was strapping on the skates, it occurred to him that he hadn't skated in years. He wondered if it was like riding a bicycle.

He managed to get across the small carpeted area. But one skate on the wood floor and he knew he was in trouble.

It took Tessa only a few moments to size up the situation.

"It's better not to hang on to the rail," she suggested. "It'll throw off your balance." She extended her free hand, while the other held Poppy's. "Let's start out slow, okay?"

He glanced backward at the benches in the carpeted area. Clearly a better choice. Then he caught Poppy's gaze. So hopeful, happy.

Morgan regretted his impulse to check on the party. He was only minutes from falling flat on his face.

Taking Tessa's hand, he forgot about the skates. Her skin was so soft, so warm, her fingers curling in between his. He swallowed, following the sensation as it hit his gut.

She was speaking but he couldn't decipher the words.

"Morgan?" Tessa repeated.

He nodded.

"So your balance *is* better?" she continued.

Realizing he wasn't flailing or falling, he tried to refocus. "Yeah."

"Good. Then we can try moving forward." Her aquamarine eyes darkened to turquoise as he continued to study them.

"Sure." Shocked, Morgan realized he didn't care if he did fall, as long as he didn't have to release her hand.

Poppy seemed to have a natural sense of balance. And Tessa was gliding along. Why was that? Stopping, he almost knocked their trio over. "You said you loved skating *as a kid*. How are you so proficient now?"

She laughed. "I don't live on skates these days

like when I was young, but I do skate when I can. In Houston I went to parks and skated on the sidewalks."

"You could have warned me."

Tessa smiled. "You're getting your balance. After you've brought Poppy here another time or two, you'll be skating like you're twelve again."

"Hmm," he replied noncommittally. There hadn't been time for outings like this. The loss of his wife knifed into him. She would have taken Poppy skating, made certain she wasn't deprived of things other children did. Thinking of her, guilt swamped him. His hand was entwined with Tessa's. What was he thinking? In a sudden move, he pulled free. Despite Tessa's excellent balance, she tumbled, taking Poppy with her.

Immediately remorseful, he knelt beside them. "Sorry."

Tessa turned to Poppy. "You okay?"

Tears welled in her eyes.

She pulled the child into her lap and stroked her hair.

Morgan's guilt multiplied. "What hurts, Poppy?"

She held out her arm.

Running her hand gently over the small arm, Tessa looked relieved. "Ah, got your elbow, huh?"

Poppy nodded.

Meeting Morgan's gaze, Tessa's expression was reassuring. "Hurts but shouldn't have any lasting effects."

"I'll take her home," Morgan announced.

"No!" Poppy wailed. "We still have cake!"

"The party's not over for a while," Tessa explained. "I can drive her home after the party breaks up."

"No, skating's too dangerous when she's still so young. I shouldn't have agreed to let her come. I don't want her hurt," Morgan insisted, wondering why Tessa thought she had a say in what Poppy could do.

"She bumped her funny bone," Tessa replied. "And if I hadn't tipped over on her, that wouldn't have happened." Tactfully, she didn't add that his pulling away had caused the fall.

Guilt threaded through his thoughts, pummeled his heart. "Can you guarantee she won't get hurt again?" He heard the hard edge in his voice but couldn't prevent it.

"Guarantee?" she asked, disbelief flashing in her eyes. Morgan flushed as he realized how absurd that sounded. Life didn't come with guarantees. He knew that better than anyone.

"How long should this cake thing take?" he asked.

"I'm not sure." She glanced across the rink. "I could ask one of the organizers."

Morgan looked at his watch, more out of habit than from a need to know the time. "I don't want her to stay too long."

It was only two o'clock in the afternoon, not the middle of the night. Wisely, Tessa didn't point out the time or his unreasonable tone. He didn't like acting the fool, and his behavior had been nothing but foolish. Mooning over holding his assistant's hand, reacting so out of character he could have seriously hurt Poppy. Even now his daughter was studying him with a puzzled look on her face, no doubt wondering what was wrong with him.

The burden on his shoulders deepened. He felt like an upside-down tower. The foundation was tiny, unsteady, and the loads that were stacked on it grew larger, more unwieldy with each layer. If he didn't watch closely, he could be facing a hostile takeover of his company, which would mean employees suddenly without jobs. Now there was also worry about Dorothy, worry that she might never fully recover. And, of course, Poppy. She needed more, not less attention than she'd had before. And Tessa seemed determined to fix that situation with trips to church and parties.

Irrationally, the feel of Tessa's hand flashed in his thoughts. She was so bent on fixing things with Poppy, he wondered if Tessa had been as fierce in trying to protect her own marriage. Even though she had worked with him for a bit now, she hadn't revealed much of herself, of her life outside of work. Had that ruined her relationship with her husband? Devoting too much of herself to her job? Was that why she was lobbying for him to spend more time with Poppy?

One thing was certain. Tessa was changing things at a rapid pace. Looking into his daughter's innocent face, Morgan felt a clutch of concern. If Poppy got too attached and Tessa decided to leave, the child would be desolate.

Chapter Eight

Morgan had conducted a fair share of interviews throughout his career. Truckers, gaugers, office staff. But none had prepared him for nannies. He understood that his small town didn't have a market for nannies and had agreed to meet with several applicants from the city. He had no prejudices against people who weren't Rosewood natives.

But he had serious issues with some of the women the agency had sent. One had spent nearly forty-five minutes trying to explain her methodology. In an awkward, unrelated transition, she was soon expounding her life philosophies. Then there was the power-hungry woman who wanted her charges to be treated like little soldiers. She was followed by two young women who were clearly more interested in men than in their work. And they weren't thrilled about the idea of relocating—asking about the single men in town. One seemed overly interested in his own availability. After several interviews his eyes were glazing over.

He thought the grandmotherly woman might be a winner. Until she fell asleep in the chair while he took a call.

Now he was down to two candidates. Neither was what he wanted, but they were the least objectionable of the lot. The casual one seemed to agree with everything he said. He had to wonder if she might be so casual she'd lose sight of Poppy or allow her to do something dangerous such as play in the street. The other, a serious woman with excellent references, worried him in another way. He didn't want a stern taskmaster for Poppy. She wasn't as forbidding as the woman with the military mannerisms, but she was awfully serious. He would have liked to see her smile more, be a little lighter. Then again the casual one smiled all the time, and bothered him for that very reason.

Finally, knowing he had to make a decision, he chose the serious candidate, Evelyn Whiting. She didn't look particularly pleased with the offer, especially when he mentioned the nanny room on the second floor. The offer of one of the cottages on the property seemed to convince her.

"I prefer having my own accommodation," she told him. "Living in the same house isn't a positive situation."

Morgan frowned. He thought living in the house would be ideal. "I'll expect you to stay in the house if I have to be gone in the evening. I work long hours."

She nodded. "That's satisfactory. However, I require one day off every weekend."

That seemed fair. Nannies rarely worked only five days, but seven was stretching it.

"And a half day during the week," she continued.

He raised his eyebrows.

"Some businesses aren't open on the weekend. Nor are dentists and doctors," she explained.

Morgan wondered if Ms. Whiting had a health problem that wasn't evident. "I suppose that could be worked out."

"Fine, then. When can I see this cottage?"

Frowning, he swallowed his distaste. He'd expected her to ask to meet Poppy. "You do understand that Poppy is only four?"

Ms. Whiting nodded. "Charges in my care have ranged from newborns to teens."

"Just know that she's accustomed to a…" He searched for a word before settling on *loose schedule*.

She frowned. "You aren't suggesting no structure, are you? A child *needs* structure. It gives them a sense of true security."

"I agree," he said, knowing that was true. "But she's had a different upbringing than most four-year-olds." He struggled to put his meaning into words. "She's used to helping Dorothy bake cookies, she works in the garden, hangs out with my assistant."

The frown on her face deepened. "You *do* employ a cook?"

"Of course. But I want Poppy to be happy."

"I do, too," Ms. Whiting replied sincerely.

He studied her. "It's been brought to my attention that she doesn't have as much contact with other children as she should."

She tipped her head. "I'll be taking her to the park. She'll get a start at interaction there."

Morgan thought of the playdates Tessa had suggested. Of course, Ms. Whiting could prove to be even more resourceful. After all she was a professional nanny. This was the best choice he could make for Poppy.

Over a week later, Morgan wasn't so sure anymore. Ms. Whiting had organized an arts and craft area in the playroom. All the supplies had been sorted and labeled. Markers were now out of Poppy's reach even though she had never misused them. But Ms. Whiting had said it set a good example.

Morgan wasn't completely convinced. The new nanny had also taken over decisions on what Poppy should wear, how the clothes were laundered, and had installed a new menu. Morgan had specifically noticed that she had also kept Poppy from Tessa's office. The little play corner sat empty. And it seemed their offices were far quieter despite the amount of work being accomplished.

So accustomed to having his daughter pop in now and then when she'd been under Dorothy's supervision, he missed her. Even Tessa seemed more reserved.

But he couldn't find any real fault in Ms. Whiting's behavior. He wished she had more warmth, but maybe that came only with a long-term or personal connection.

Tessa strolled in, her eyes fixed downward on the envelope she carried. "Another delivery." She shifted the envelope, gauging its weight. "Feels like it could be logs." She referred to the drilling logs that recorded the progress on an active well Harper Petroleum was invested in.

"I'm expecting two new surveys," Morgan remembered. "Ones that need to go to Houston."

Tessa glanced at her watch. "We could still get another delivery. It's only five o'clock."

"Only? You've been here since seven."

"And you've been here since…?"

"We didn't break for lunch," he suddenly remembered. Dorothy would have made sure they stopped.

"I didn't realize," Tessa replied.

"We can have an early dinner," Morgan suggested. "I can talk to…"

"Nancy," she supplied.

He glanced out at the empty hallway.

"Ms. Whiting has Poppy practicing her letters," Tessa told him, guessing the direction of his thoughts.

"Oh."

"It's something they usually learn at preschool. Dorothy's already taught her the alphabet, but I was going to suggest the Rainbow class as a way to get her more time with other kids."

"Ms. Whiting says she'll do that at the park."

"Oh," Tessa echoed. "I'm sure that will work."

They both glanced toward the still-empty hallway.

"Well, I'd better get back to my desk," she said finally.

The promise of an early dinner forgotten, he turned back to his computer. Within an hour the doorbell rang.

Tessa answered the door, as had been her habit since Dorothy's stroke.

Morgan heard her voice and another.

"This might be the other delivery you're expecting," she said only moments later.

Eager to study the new properties, Morgan blotted out everything else. He didn't notice when Tessa left to join Poppy for dinner around six, nor her return only thirty minutes later. One of the new surveys looked extremely promising. He dropped it in his briefcase, intending to take it to Houston in a few minutes. His geologist was driving in from the field to meet him in the city.

He put the other survey in his bottom drawer. Glancing at his watch, he had his hands up when Poppy rushed into the office, plowing directly into him.

"Whoa..." His voice trailed away as he realized she was sobbing. Swiftly he knelt down. "Sweetheart, what is it?" he asked, running his hands quickly over her arms and legs, looking for some injury.

"Daddy!" she wailed.

On a run, Tessa erupted from her office. "Poppy!" Halting, she dropped down, crouching beside them, looking to Morgan for answers. "What is it?"

"I don't know," Morgan replied, pulling Poppy into his lap. "Tell me what's wrong."

"Fr-Freckles!" she managed between gulps.

"Something happened to Freckles?" he questioned, hoping only the stuffed dog was harmed and not his daughter.

"What happened?" Tessa asked, unable to remain silent.

"She...she put him up."

"Up?" Morgan and Tessa echoed together.

"She said I didn't need him to sleep with me. I told her Freckles would be scared without me."

Morgan pulled her even closer, kissing the top of her head. "I will get Freckles and he can be with you whenever you want. Tessa, while we go retrieve Freckles, would you ask Ms. Whiting to wait here in my study." It wasn't a question.

Tessa nodded, reaching out to pat Poppy's arm and give her a smile. Then she met his gaze and he saw a well of understanding in her eyes.

Nearing the staircase, Morgan stalked past the nanny, who started to follow. Behind him he heard a blend of voices, Tessa's sounding firmer than he'd ever heard it.

Upstairs, he saw that Ms. Whiting had put Freckles on top of the armoire in Poppy's room, far too high for her to ever reach the toy. Anger continued to multiply the more he thought of the heartless action. Carrying Poppy across the room, he placed her in bed, then retrieved Freckles. Lucy had bought the stuffed animal for her daughter after she'd first learned she was pregnant. When Poppy had latched on to it, Morgan had sensed a connection beyond the earthly realm.

Tears still streaked Poppy's flushed cheeks.

"I think Freckles could use a hug," he suggested, handing her the well-loved, well-worn toy.

She clutched her precious stuffed dog. "He didn't like being up so high."

Morgan nodded seriously. "Of course not. We won't ever put him up there again."

"What about Ms. Whiting?"

His lips tightened. Just then he heard a discreet cough at the door. Glancing up, he saw that it was Tessa.

She smiled tentatively. "I've missed seeing Poppy to bed this week. Do you think I could have a few minutes with her?"

He was more than ready to take on the nanny. Remarkable that his assistant had guessed he wanted to deal with the woman immediately.

Downstairs, Ms. Whiting began protesting as soon as he reached the study. "You're spoiling that child, the way she runs willy-nilly all over the place. There's no structure in that sort of upbringing."

"And there's no love in yours." Morgan felt the heat of his fury. "You won't be getting a letter of recommendation from me."

She drew herself up in the chair. "I have more than enough references without yours."

He narrowed his eyes. "Which you pick and cull, I imagine. I know I'm not the only parent who disapproves of your methods. I want you cleared out tomorrow. If you weren't living on the property, I'd want you out tonight. I will be talking to your agency."

Anger twisted her mouth, but she restrained herself, bristling as she stood from the chair, then marching out of the study.

A sick ugliness twisted in Morgan's gut. He wished Alvin was still on watch. He'd have made sure the woman was gone swiftly. Morgan had not been able to hire a temporary replacement for all the duties and responsibilities Alvin took care of. Morgan had settled for now on hiring a lawn service and a window washer. But Alvin did so much more, including keeping tabs on the property, making sure it was secure. Morgan wouldn't feel right until Ms. Whiting was gone.

He glanced at his watch. The survey he'd chosen needed to get to Houston, but as much as he appreciated Tessa's assistance with Poppy, he didn't want to leave his daughter. Not tonight. Not after what Ms. Whiting had done to her.

Climbing the curving stairs, he felt the quiet in the house. Having always resonated with several voices, it seemed different somehow, yet not as lonely as he expected. Rugs carpeted the wood floor in the long hallway on the landing. Reaching Poppy's room, he paused. Gentle, lulling strains of a child's song lilted through the air. Tessa sang softly, sweetly.

He peeked around the corner and saw Tessa brush Poppy's hair back from her forehead. Tessa made no signs of moving, no impatience. Instead she lifted her hand to her mouth, then carefully placed the kiss on her fingertips to Poppy's cheek. As he watched, frozen in place, her voice grew softer until it finally faded away. Standing, she clicked the lamp so that only the night-light portion remained lit.

She spotted him as she turned. He put one finger to his lips. Not speaking, she followed him out of Poppy's room.

"Door open?" she asked. "Just in case she has any dreams?"

"I think so. Dorothy has the hearing of a bat, always knew when Poppy cried as soon as I did."

"She's missed in so many ways."

He swallowed. "And I haven't done a very good job of providing for Poppy, certainly not the way Dorothy would have wanted."

Tessa placed her hand on his arm, warming his skin. "She would be proud of the way you've handled things. We have a great cook and housekeeper—not as great as Dorothy, but who is? And you did your best hiring Ms. Whiting. She didn't appear to have a mean streak. People can hide that sort of thing pretty well. She's made a career of it."

He shook his head. "I couldn't have hired anyone much worse."

"You can talk to the agency tomorrow, clue them in on Ms. Whiting and see if they have someone else," Tessa suggested.

"I'll do that, but supposedly they sent the best candidates the first time." Morgan shrugged. "We can play it by ear."

She looked down. "We weren't doing too badly before Ms. Whiting took over."

"Good way to put it," he realized. "She *did* take over. I don't know why I let her."

"Because she was supposed to be the expert?" Tessa suggested.

"Being Poppy's father should make me even more qualified, shouldn't it?"

Tessa smiled, something she didn't do often enough. But when she did, a little fizzle of something inexplicable ripped through him. Her smile erased all the professionalism, the efficiency, the distance. Only inches from her face, he could see that her smile was artless, as natural as breathing. Why had she stopped smiling? Had the divorce she never talked about hurt her so much it had stolen her smiles?

"Daddy!" A sudden wail filled the air.

They broke apart. Even though Tessa's touch was light, he felt a physical separation when her hand dropped away.

Together they rushed back to Poppy, perching on each side of her.

"What is it?" Morgan asked, surprised she'd awakened so quickly.

Tessa rubbed Poppy's shoulder in a comforting gesture.

"I thought you left!" Poppy wailed.

He remembered the survey that needed to go to Houston.

"I can take the packet to the city," Tessa offered, apparently reading his thoughts.

"Don't go, Tessa," Poppy pleaded.

She stared helplessly at Morgan for direction. The surveys were confidential. He hadn't wanted to involve anyone else in their transfer. If competitors got a whiff of the land he was considering, he could be undercut or outbid. He ran a mental roster of people at work he implicitly trusted. One of them could ferry the packet this time. And he could phone his geologist, ask him to study the survey, then postpone their meeting.

"Don't worry. We'll both be here," Morgan promised. "I'll get someone from the office to make the trip tonight."

"Would you like a story?" Tessa asked Poppy, smoothing the blanket.

Poppy nodded. *"Cinderella."*

Tessa's smile was soft, gentle. "One of my favorites."

"While Tessa reads to you, I've got to make a phone call," Morgan told his daughter. "But I'll be here. You don't have anything to be scared of."

Tessa, book in hand, sat back down on the bed.

Not quite sure why, he trusted that Poppy would be okay with Tessa. He needed to phone Janet, get the errand set up so he could concentrate on his daughter. He could trust Janet. They went back a long way.

Dependable as always, Janet agreed to make sure the packet was delivered that night. She had always been dedicated. After Lucy died, Janet had helped deflect some of the business strain, accepting condolences on his behalf, condolences he couldn't bear to hear. He knew his business associates were only being kind, considerate, but each word of sympathy had been like a new nail pounded into his heart.

Because of Janet's dedication, Morgan had promoted her. Knowing how heavy a load she was carrying, he had authorized an assistant for her, one he trusted Janet to hire. The woman she'd chosen, Sherry Richardson, had become an asset, as well. He needed to remind Tessa that one of them could help with her workload, freeing her up to spend time with Poppy at least until he could find a trustworthy nanny, if one existed. Common sense told him if he lived in a city large enough to have a market for nannies, his task would be easy. But finding someone willing to relocate to a small town far from big-city attractions narrowed his selection considerably.

So he was back to where he started. He glanced upward, thinking of Tessa, recognizing that she had an intuitive connection with Poppy. A connection that he could nurture or deflect. Remembering the warmth of her touch, he didn't know which course was wiser.

Chapter Nine

Poppy clung close to Tessa in the days following Ms. Whiting's departure. She was eager to leap into her father's arms, but when he was away working, she became Tessa's shadow.

Tessa didn't mind. She loved spending time with the sweet child. And she appreciated Morgan's offer of extra help while they were without a nanny. Tessa was fine with doing double duty, but Morgan's work took her at least ten hours a day, hours she now had to split with Poppy.

Janet and Sherry sat in Tessa's office, each with a computer tablet, taking notes.

Poppy studied them from the safety of her corner. Since Ms. Whiting's malicious actions, Poppy was a little more reserved. Tessa felt sure that would lessen in time, but she didn't blame the child. Having only known love, meanness had been an assault.

"What brought you to Rosewood?" Sherry asked, chewing her gum as enthusiastically as she typed.

"This is a great job," Tessa replied, not ready

to confide her full situation to this stranger. Both Sherry and Janet seemed nice, but Tessa had always been a private person. She'd told Morgan the reason but didn't want to discuss her divorce with people she'd just met. She didn't truly want to talk about it with anyone. A flash of pain registered. Keeping busy with Poppy pushed much of her torment away. There were times when she didn't think of Karl, of what he'd said, until deep in the night when she was alone. On days that were completely filled with work and Poppy, her thoughts had taken a different turn. The man she dwelled on was Morgan.

"And Morgan's a great boss," Janet filled in when there was a sudden silence.

"So you know him well?" Tessa replied.

Janet glanced down. Sherry lifted her eyebrows and her lips twitched.

"Did I say something wrong?" Tessa asked.

"Of course not," Janet replied. "Sherry's thinking about some ancient history. Morgan and I dated when we were in high school. No big deal."

"Not the way I heard it," Sherry murmured.

Tessa glanced at Janet, who hesitated. "We were the king and queen of the prom," Janet explained. "It's a small town, so people made assumptions."

Though curious, Tessa resisted the urge to ask more. She didn't want to seem like a gossip, especially about her boss. So she steered the conversational direction in another path. "I've never lived in a small town before. I'm from Houston."

"The town's a living thing all its own," Janet agreed. "We do tend to know most everybody."

"And their business," Sherry added. "That's how I know about Janet and Morgan." The woman seemed determined to concentrate on one particular bit of that business.

"Past tense." Janet tapped her tablet, pulling up another screen. "If you're agreeable," she began, "we can start tomorrow and we can adjust to your schedule. I'll email you a copy of my calendar and you can tell me what will work best."

"Sounds very doable," Tessa agreed. "If Morgan gets a nanny hired sooner than he thinks, I might not need the help for long."

"We're flexible," Janet responded.

"Yes," Sherry agreed. "Look…" She hesitated. "I wasn't trying to be difficult. Once you've lived here awhile you'll see what I mean about small towns. Has its good points, as well."

"Are you a native?" Tessa questioned.

Sherry shook her head. "No. My husband's job brought us here. Kind of like you. Didn't you work for a big oil company in Houston?"

"Yes."

Sherry waited expectantly.

So Tessa complied. "Traxton."

"Great company, probably a lot different than working for a small independent."

"It's an interesting contrast," Tessa concluded.

Janet clicked off her tablet and stood. "We'd better get back to the office. Good to actually meet you, Tessa. One of these days we'll get you in to visit the main office."

"I'd like that," Tessa responded, walking with them to the door, bidding them goodbye.

"How come you didn't like that gum lady?" Poppy asked.

"What makes you think I didn't like her?"

Poppy tipped her small head. "Did you?"

"We don't want to be unkind, do we?"

Poppy scrunched her face. "I'm not."

"Okay, then."

Tessa glanced over at Morgan's empty desk. In trying to catch up, he had been gone all day.

The days that followed slid one into another. Morgan was gone the next day, then the next until the week stuttered to an end.

By Saturday evening, Tessa made a decision, hoping it wasn't a fateful one. Morgan wasn't around to ask, so she decided that she would take Poppy with her to church the next day. Again she worried about the amount of time he spent away from Poppy. But she knew Sunday school and church would be good for the child.

Morgan got home late Saturday evening. Tessa had made up the bed in the nanny's room that was next to Poppy's, having slept in it most of the week while Morgan was gone. Although she loved her little cottage, it wasn't set up too well for company. There was a small second bedroom but Tessa had spent all of her time either working or with Poppy, never getting an opportunity to do much with the space. And Poppy slept best in her own bed.

Tessa was nearly asleep when she heard the quiet footfalls in the hallway. She had left the connecting door to the nursery open, and she watched as Morgan approached, smoothed the covers, then gently kissed Poppy's forehead.

Pulling back her own covers, she was ready to talk to him about attending church the following morning. Then she heard it. A sigh that was heavy, heartfelt. Even in the dim light, she could see that he was exhausted. And she couldn't bring herself to confront him. There was always the morning, when they'd both be better rested. Not that falling asleep seemed very likely. Certainly not when she kept picturing Morgan's face, the set of his deep brown eyes, firm lips and strong jaw. All put together in a way she couldn't ignore.

By morning, Tessa had battled with her sheets and blanket until they were a twisted, sad heap. And she was ready for a reprieve. Peeking into Poppy's room, she could see that the child was still asleep. She sped to her cottage for a quick shower and change of clothes.

Poppy was still asleep when Tessa returned. "Wake up, sleepyhead."

Poppy's eyes popped open, shining like new pennies. "You're all dressed up."

"Just a dress," Tessa replied. "It's Sunday."

"Sunny school!" Poppy threw back the covers, dancing on the bed. "Yay!"

"I haven't asked your father yet," Tessa cautioned, knowing her plans could easily be quashed.

But Poppy was already pulling open the closet door.

Deciding to get the child ready, Tessa figured she could take on Morgan if he protested.

"I have a yellow dress," Poppy announced. She scooted across the room to an antique white dresser and pulled open a drawer. "I have new socks, too."

Tessa helped her into the frock, rounded up dressy shoes and looked for a barrette. Finding only tiny elastic hair bands, she frowned. "Where are your barrettes and hair bows?"

Poppy shrugged.

It occurred to Tessa that Morgan wouldn't think to buy any. She knew Dorothy had bought the two dresses, dress socks and shoes. Usually Poppy was outfitted in T-shirts and shorts or jeans. Evidently it hadn't occurred to Morgan or Dorothy that she needed a few more *girlie* things. Tessa added barrettes and hair bows to her mental shopping list.

She brushed Poppy's soft blond hair, loving the silky texture. So pretty, she thought, wishing for a bow to adorn the curls. Not wanting to be late, she checked Poppy's outfit.

"Am I okay?" Poppy asked seriously.

"More than okay. You're perfect." She took Poppy's hand. "Ready for breakfast?"

"Uh-huh." Trust poured from the tiny fisted fingers into Tessa's and she felt a hitch that had nothing to do with her job or responsibilities.

She didn't hear a peep from Morgan while they were upstairs nor in the kitchen, where they ate bowls of cereal. Nancy came in for only a few hours on every other Sunday and Heather was off. Poppy considered cereal a treat since Dorothy didn't serve it often, instead always cooking a hot breakfast. Tessa reached halfway through her own bowl and paused. When had much of her appetite returned?

Morgan still hadn't come downstairs, so Tessa wrote two notes explaining where they were. One she attached to the refrigerator door and the other she taped to his office chair, where it couldn't be missed.

Expecting to be stopped any moment, told she could not take Poppy to church, it turned out to be rather anticlimactic when the morning went smoothly. Morgan didn't appear before they left.

Poppy was excited to go to Sunday school and then junior church. But Tessa decided not to push it when Cindy invited them to lunch. She didn't want to return to Morgan pacing up and down.

To her surprise, Morgan wasn't waiting for them when they returned. After changing out of their dresses, Tessa made French toast, one of Poppy's favorites. She had checked the office but Morgan was nowhere in sight.

Deciding she had to let Morgan know where they'd been, she texted him.

He didn't reply.

Thinking that was ominous, she waited while they ate, but nothing showed up on her phone. As she checked it, the ringtone suddenly played. Slightly startled, she pushed Answer.

"I'm in Jefferson," he greeted her.

"Problems with the pipeline construction?" she guessed.

"Ronnie called around three in the morning."

Standing, she turned so that Poppy wouldn't hear. "I was worried when you seemed to have disappeared."

"Didn't you find my note?" he questioned.

"Note?"

"On your desk."

"Oh. I haven't been in my office. It's *Sunday*."

"I noticed." His voice was even.

She waited. Another few seconds passed and she couldn't stay still. "I had planned to ask you first."

More silence.

"But you weren't around," she finished in a rush.

"Planning any other unauthorized maneuvers?"

She felt herself flushing.

"I'm guessing you're not going to say what you think," he continued. "I should be home by dinnertime. I trust you won't have swooped Poppy off to Dallas by then."

Tessa clutched her phone. "Poppy's expecting to ride Cornflake today."

He muttered but she couldn't make out the words. "Was that your idea, too?"

"It was yours," she reminded him crisply, referring to a promise he'd made shortly after she'd come to work for him.

"So it was." He exhaled. "I'll be there soon. I'll take the plane."

Something twisted in her gut. "I hate those little planes. So many crash."

"I don't intend to."

"No one ever does." She couldn't keep the words inside, even though she knew she was over the line.

"See you soon."

A few hours later, Morgan pulled up in front of his house. He'd taken a company pickup truck from the airport, having left his own SUV in Jefferson. It would be easy enough to get his vehicle back. Harper did a lot of business in East Texas. Someone could bring it back on a return trip.

The pickup from the airport was a basic truck. No frills, no accessories. Gaugers used them as they drove to and from the pipelines. With the exception of an extra fuel tank, the truck was as bare as possible.

"I want to sit by the window!" Poppy announced.

Morgan looked at Tessa. That would put her in the middle. He had been surprised when Poppy insisted on having Tessa come along when they went riding. But he couldn't refuse without being rude. Not that he wanted to refuse. Wishing he could dispatch his thoughts, Morgan slid onto the bench seat.

Tessa and Poppy joined him. Although Poppy didn't take up much space, she was wriggling around in her excitement, bumping into Tessa, bumping Tessa into him.

The first time she brushed against him, Tessa stiffened her arm and side, but the posture was difficult to maintain. He drove through the neighborhood, then past downtown. Before they reached the main highway, he turned down a dirt road that was a shortcut to the stable. When the truck hit the first rut, Tessa bounced over the seat, struggling to maintain her position. Poppy liked the bouncing, adding her own energy to the action the truck was making.

Morgan glanced down at Tessa, catching her gaze. Her aquamarine eyes darkened. Jewels, he thought. Caged jewels.

A deep rut caused the truck to veer sharply to the right. Morgan wrenched the steering wheel to get them back on course. Tessa cleared her throat but didn't say anything.

He liked the soft feel of her beside him. She'd changed into jeans and a cotton shirt, but she looked just as pretty as when she was wearing one of her classy suits or dresses. There was something beautifully natural about her looks. Not that her eyes were ones he'd seen on anyone else. Remarkably different. *Lovely.*

The word popped into his thoughts like a shot.

Sneaking a look, he liked the casual ponytail that held her dark hair at the nape of her neck. It looked as though it would be soft to the touch.

"Daddy?"

Reality returned with a thud. "Yes?" His voice was thick.

"Can Tessa ride Beauty?"

He swallowed. Beauty had been Lucy's horse. He couldn't bear to ride her but he couldn't part with her, either. So friends took her out, making sure the mare didn't feel neglected. But Morgan was never at the stables when they did. He hadn't thought about which horse Tessa would ride when they'd all agreed to go. The stable rented horses.

And fortunately, his father had always kept extra horses so that he could entertain visiting business guests from the city. A ride through the picturesque Hill Country softened many a tough customer. Currently, they owned five horses, his own—Duke—plus Cornflake, Beauty, Peaches and Tora.

The building was just past the upcoming hill. The dirt road continued though a fallow field that was dominated by tall wild grass and strewn with buttercups and bluebonnets, a flurry of wildflowers.

Stopping off to one side, he put the truck into Park, then leaned against the steering wheel for a few moments. "Okay, let's get going."

As they approached the adjoining stalls, he could hear Duke neigh as he caught their scent. Morgan patted Duke's neck, eliciting a return gesture as Duke lifted his massive head up, then down again.

Suddenly he was hit with what should have been his first thought. "Tessa, do you ride?"

She smiled. "I'd have mentioned it if I didn't. But it's been a while. My horse is stabled at my parents' house."

He frowned. "I thought they lived in the city."

"Close. On twenty acres in Magnolia."

Quite a drive, but by Houston standards, it wasn't far. "You haven't mentioned owning a horse."

Tessa shrugged. "It never came up."

"This is Cornflake," Poppy announced, stroking her pony's mane.

"He looks just the color of a cornflake," Tessa commented, smiling at Poppy.

Morgan liked the way she spoke *to* Poppy rather than down *at* her. Poppy obviously liked it, as well.

Beauty, standing in the next stall, whinnied for attention. He moved over, stroking her fawn-colored mane. It made perfect sense to let Tessa ride her.

But he just couldn't. The horse was inextricably tied to his memories of Lucy.

So he moved on to pat Peaches. "This girl will give you a good ride," he told Tessa.

"Her name is Peaches," Poppy added, still caught up with her own horse.

"Peaches? I like that." Tessa moved next to him, reaching out to stroke the horse, as well. "You're a pretty girl."

A fine chestnut mare, Morgan reasoned. Peaches was an excellent horse. And hopefully, Poppy wouldn't mention Beauty again.

He went to the tack room and picked one of his saddles for Tessa. The tack room was always open and every sort of saddle was stored inside. It was something people outside Rosewood didn't understand. They expected theft, especially of the more expensive items, but everything stayed intact, safe.

He hefted the saddle onto Peaches.

Tessa quickly took her place beside him. "I can cinch her up."

"You said you hadn't ridden for a while."

"But I remember how to saddle a horse."

Reluctantly he stepped aside, ready to move in if he was needed. But Tessa had a good handle on what she was doing. He shouldn't be surprised. She was amazingly competent. She'd learned the job without one hiccup, was intuitive to the point that she knew what he needed before he voiced it. In addition she'd fitted right into the household, winning Poppy's favor immediately, Dorothy's, as well.

He lifted Poppy's saddle, helping her, reinforcing her actions, making certain everything was securely cinched. Then he attended to Duke's saddle.

Leading the horses out of the stable, they paused so he could give Poppy a hand up. He turned to Tessa but she effortlessly mounted Peaches, leaning forward to pat the horse's mane and speak quietly to her. He wouldn't be surprised if she turned out to be a prize-winning equestrian.

Morgan took the lead toward the meadows that led up the hills. Slowing, he settled in beside Poppy as they rode three abreast in the seemingly endless field.

"I'm surprised this isn't more built up," Tessa commented as she surveyed the miles of rolling land.

"It's in private hands," Morgan explained. "You know that in Rosewood we like keeping the big chains out, developers, too. So we have the space to leave land undeveloped, since the established businesses here already have all the space they need. The businesses are owned locally, so they thrive all through the year, not just during wildflower season. We don't have spikes in housing demands, either. Too many towns are filled with hotels, restaurants, T-shirt and souvenir shops. We aren't interested in living like that."

"So you're against any kind of change?"

"Nope. We move with the times. But that doesn't mean you can't hold on to tradition and values. We like homegrown businesses instead of superstores. During wildflower season, it's fair to say our bed-and-breakfast is booked. But that's okay. We're not opposed to visitors, just don't want to be a one-stop town."

"I guess I hadn't looked at it that way. Although I've tried to buy American for as long as I can remember. It's something my parents drilled into me.

That it wasn't worth saving a quarter on something manufactured overseas when that quarter might mean someone over here was going to lose their job."

Morgan nodded. "Sound like sensible people."

"I'm fond of them," she replied drily, her lips twitching.

"Do you miss them?" He hadn't meant to ask, but there it was. He wondered about the life she'd abandoned.

"Of course, but even when I was in Houston, I lived in the Galleria area."

The Galleria, the place many successful career people in Houston radiated to. Hip, chic, hot, it was a coveted area. He also knew that it was a good drive from there to Magnolia.

"So," she continued, "I didn't see my parents as much as you'd think."

"Too bad," he replied, remembering how he had enjoyed having his parents close.

"They retired in Magnolia," she explained. "They've always wanted to get out of the city, leave Houston behind. But I'm an only child and they weren't keen on being far away. Of course, now Houston's growing right into Magnolia. You know how Houston spreads out." The city had devoured communities in every direction, annexing hundreds of miles.

"But you still chose to move away?" Morgan questioned.

Tessa glanced over at Poppy as though she didn't

want the child to hear too much. "They understood. It was a...time—" she swallowed "—that needed change. You're an only child, yet your parents are traveling. It's kind of the same principle. Our lives will intersect forever but they can't always follow the same road."

He considered her words in silence as they rode toward the hills. When the trail began a steady, up-hill incline, Tessa looked more and more apprehensive.

"Something wrong?" Morgan asked.

"I have a problem with heights," she admitted. "I didn't realize we'd be climbing this much."

He looked at the relatively mild incline. "It gets higher. Is that going to be a problem?"

She gripped her reins more tightly. "Probably."

"At the next switchback, we'll turn around." He watched her closely until they reached the space. Even though they headed downhill, she still looked worried. "Won't be long before we're down."

"Coming down is usually the hardest part," she admitted. "I feel as though I could tip forward and roll down the rest of the way."

"Your horse won't let you," Morgan reassured her.

"Does Peaches know that?" Tessa muttered.

Hearing her, Morgan realized how frightened she was. He would have to remember that for future rides. There were plenty of riding paths on flat ground.

The wind picked up a bit, ruffling Tessa's hair. But

she'd pulled it back in a ponytail that kept it manageable. Poppy, however, had hair blowing into her face.

"Is something wrong with your ponytail band?" he asked.

"I don't have it on," Poppy replied, shaking her head to get the hair from her face.

"Why not?"

She frowned, unusual for her. "I don't like them."

Morgan glanced at Tessa. "Do you know what she's talking about?"

"There are different types of barrettes and ponytail clips," she explained diplomatically as they neared the flat ground, her grip on the reins a little looser. "There might be a kind she'd like better."

"Wouldn't a rubber band work?"

Tessa winced. "It would tangle and pull her hair. She needs something that will work on soft baby hair."

"Dorothy's always bought them and I don't know anything about barrettes." He held up his hand as though balancing an invisible, unwieldy ball.

"I imagine Dorothy was used to one kind from when she was younger and may have never had long hair. Be easy to check out what the stores have, see if another kind of barrette will work better for Poppy."

Morgan glanced at his daughter. "Poppy, can you keep on riding?"

"Sure, Daddy." She shook her head again, letting the hair fall back from her face. "Cornflake misses me when I'm not here to ride him."

He exchanged an unexpected smile with Tessa. The movement changed her entire face. Always pretty, Tessa glowed when she smiled. It was as though whatever held the clamp on her feelings eased up, allowing the real Tessa to surface.

Morgan wondered at his own fancy. Women didn't render him poetic. At least none other than Lucy. And that trait had died with her.

Tessa glanced toward Poppy, her smile growing. And he felt the punch in his heart. Was it his past talking, warning him? Or was it… The notion unsettled him. No, it couldn't be more.

Chapter Ten

Monday morning dawned, a clear, bright new day.

Poppy bounced into Morgan's study. She made a direct line for Tessa, who sat across the desk from him.

"Daddy said I can have new barrettes."

"You remember," Morgan explained, embarrassed that he hadn't noticed that his daughter needed new barrettes before. He had no clue what Poppy liked to wear, which was why Dorothy or his mother had bought all of her clothes. "We need something to keep the hair out of her face when she's riding, but I don't know anything about barrettes."

"A trip to the store should tell us what's available."

Morgan shook his head. "I'm not sure—"

"Don't look so appalled. I'll be glad to take Poppy shopping." Tessa looked at Poppy. "How does that sound?"

Poppy grinned. "Can we go now?"

"I have to work," Tessa explained. "But I really

need a helper. One who likes to work with paper clips. I wonder where I could find somebody like that."

"Me! Me! I like paper clips!" Poppy's exuberance was contagious. "Can we use the colored ones?"

Morgan wondered how Tessa concentrated with his little bundle of energy parked in her office.

"Let's get you settled in my office so I can go over any notes your dad has for me."

Morgan shook his head. "You're free on this end. I have some things lined up and I need to meet with Ronnie Broussard."

"Anything wrong?"

"Routine. Repair updates, new line to Jefferson." He stopped. "Why don't you take Poppy to the store today? I'll need you most of tomorrow."

"I don't want to take advantage…"

"You're taking care of Poppy. I'd say the ledger's balanced on your side." Opening his wallet, he pulled out a credit card. "Pay with this."

"I don't mind buying a few barrettes and things," she argued.

"It's the *things* I'm worried about. No arguments."

"I'm not arguing," she replied. But the gleam in her eyes was at odds with her words.

Even so, he couldn't quash Poppy's excitement. Tessa was keeping Poppy's mind off Dorothy. The hospital was his first stop today. To see if Dorothy had improved. And to spell Alvin.

Best of all, it would get him out of the house and away from Tessa. Yesterday's ride had created more questions than answers, unnerving him. How had he let this situation develop?

Tessa felt as though she'd fallen down the rabbit hole, emerging with a whole new identity. She loved the entire process of picking out hair bows, socks, two new dresses, tights and a cute skirt set for Poppy. Now they were trying to choose a purse. Poppy was torn between two. Feeling as though it was Christmas, Tessa impulsively decided to buy both. She didn't plan to use Morgan's credit card. This shopping trip was her treat.

It didn't take long to determine Poppy wasn't a spoiled child. She was excited over each item. However, Tessa was surprised when Poppy lingered at a display of necklaces.

"These are for grown-ups," Tessa explained.

Poppy nodded solemnly, fingering one with a butterfly design. "Dorothy likes butterflies."

"You want this for Dorothy?"

"Uh-huh," Poppy replied solemnly.

Tessa didn't know when Poppy would be allowed to see Dorothy. "Tell you what. We'll go ahead and buy the necklace for Dorothy, but you still have to wait to see her until your dad says it's okay. No badgering him to go before he thinks you should."

Poppy met her eyes, her brow crinkled. "Okay. But I can still ask him, right?"

"Of course. But the necklace will be tucked away until it's the right time to visit Dorothy." Tessa understood Morgan's wish to protect Poppy, to post-pone any visits until Dorothy looked healthier. She guessed Dorothy felt the same way, not wanting to frighten her favorite little girl.

Tessa worried about Dorothy. Morgan had dis-couraged her from visiting, as well. He had told her flatly that Dorothy's condition was too bad for vis-itors. She was being well looked after by a small army of doctors, technicians and therapists. And Morgan felt she and Alvin needed their time alone. His own visits were quick, except when spelling Alvin. Although Morgan had secured a private visi-tors' room for Alvin, the older man preferred sleep-ing on a recliner in Dorothy's room. He wanted to be at her side, not even five minutes away. Tessa could tell that Morgan was worried about Alvin as well as Dorothy.

Poppy interrupted her thoughts. "Is it going to be a really long time till I see Dorothy?"

Tessa squatted so that she could evenly meet the child's eyes. "I hope not. I know she misses you."

Poppy frowned. "Daddy said she can't talk. How do you know she misses me?"

Reaching out impulsively, Tessa hugged her. "Be-cause you're so special she *must* be missing you."

Poppy hugged her back. "I'm glad you're here."

"Me, too," Tessa confided. "Me, too."

The week passed and Morgan saw a note of hope in Dorothy's condition. The speech therapist's work was paying off. And there was a spark in Dorothy's eyes, one that had been missing since the onset of her stroke.

The continued building of the new pipeline in Jefferson kept Morgan busy and out of the house much of the time. Between work and time at the hospital, the days flew past. Suddenly it was Saturday.

He still hadn't resolved the unexpected feelings Tessa had stirred when they'd gone riding. He wondered if she had chosen him as her project of sorts—a lost lamb she needed to bring back to God. He hadn't been around to deny Poppy a trip to church the previous Sunday. But now he needed to put a stop to the practice. It was time to let Tessa know he was serious. He didn't intend to be mean-spirited, but Poppy's future demanded the truth. He didn't want her relying on a faith that wouldn't protect her.

There had been a time when he could never have envisioned losing his own faith. He had turned all important matters over to God, trusting things to come out right.

But there was no justification in Lucy's death.

Generous, kind, loving, she was the personification of all things good in the world. There could be no benefit in her loss, no test to be won or lost, no higher purpose to be served. She was simply gone. From her family, from him. From their daughter.

He didn't want Poppy to grow up believing that faith would keep pain and loss away. He'd rather she stuck to fairy tales. At least she knew those were just make-believe stories.

The doorbell rang, startling him out of his thoughts.

In moments, Tessa handed him a packet that had just come by delivery.

He opened the envelope. "The newest surveys."

She nodded.

Morgan scanned the first survey, then thought about the next day, Sunday, and how he was going to keep Poppy from attending church. He made a sudden decision. "We're going to have to work tomorrow."

"All day?" Tessa questioned.

"All day." He waited for the protest.

"Starting at seven or eight o'clock?"

"Eight. It is Sunday." An unnecessary reminder.

He expected her to say something, anything. To protest, actually, but she didn't utter a word.

The following morning, Tessa carried two cups of coffee into the office, balancing them so she could flick on the lights. Even though Morgan wasn't in his office yet, he could show up in seconds.

The previous night she'd thought hard, prayed even harder. With the courage she'd sustained from that, she had phoned Cindy. Her friend didn't hesitate.

But Tessa was far less certain of Morgan's reaction. She put the mug with a bit of sugar on his desk, then entered her own space. Keeping up with her work was daunting while spending so much time with Poppy. All week after she'd helped Poppy bathe, then settle in bed with a story and song, she had retreated to her office to finish what she'd left undone during the day, the tasks that hadn't been delegated to Janet or Sherry. Morgan got Poppy up in the mornings, so she was able to get in more work before they came downstairs. Still, she was giving more and more of her work to Janet and Sherry.

Just as she settled in her chair, the house phone rang. Expecting it, Tessa stilled her hands to listen. It rang four times. Heather was off since she didn't work Sundays. And Nancy rarely answered the phone. Tessa had counted on that.

On the fifth ring, someone picked up the phone. Tessa couldn't hear any voices, so Morgan must still be upstairs. The minutes crawled by before she heard heavy footsteps on the stairs. He paused in the circular entry hall, then headed toward the office.

But she didn't hear the creak of his chair, which meant he was probably walking on the thick rug. His appearance in her office confirmed the guess.

"Morning," she greeted him. "There's fresh coffee on your desk."

"Fine."

She swallowed, wishing he would get to the point. "I added sugar," she said inanely.

"Were you on the phone early this morning, Tessa?"

"No," she replied truthfully. She'd spoken to Cindy the previous evening.

"Funny. Cindy just called. Her words sounded as though you'd written her script."

"Well, we are old friends…"

"Don't you want to know why she called?"

Tessa gripped her mug. "Sure."

"She invited Poppy to go to Sunday school with her kids."

"They're great kids," Tessa managed.

"I know what kind of kids they are. But why did Cindy suddenly decide to invite Poppy? Something she's never done before?"

Tessa considered her options. Waffling, fibbing or the truth. She lifted her chin. "Because I'm working and can't take Poppy."

"I didn't give you permission to take her today."

"I didn't ask."

"Don't quibble about technicalities."

"Hardly. I *was* going to ask you last night, but there wasn't much point once I knew I'd have to work." Some of the confidence she'd lost because of Karl struggled to be heard. "What did you tell Cindy?"

Morgan narrowed his gaze, and she had the distinct feeling he could read her thoughts. "I'm letting Poppy go."

Tessa started to smile.

"That's because Poppy overheard our conversation and I didn't want her to feel excluded. Don't you realize what a bad position you've put me in? First over the party, now today. I won't tolerate having you turn my child against me."

Shocked, she stared at him. "You don't really believe I'm trying to do that?" Dismay filled her. "I just want to help Poppy. It's obvious she adores you. Nothing's going to change that. Being involved with other children will be good for her. So will going to church. It won't change your relationship."

Abruptly she stood, gripping the desk with shaking fingers. "If I'm giving you the impression that I have ulterior motives regarding Poppy, I…I think I should resign." Tessa couldn't meet his eyes, afraid hers might fill with the tears she never allowed in front of anyone. "Janet at the main office is thorough. I'm sure she could help out until you find someone else, someone more…suited."

"Don't fall on your sword," Morgan muttered before exhaling. "Look, I don't want you to quit. But I do want you to stop going behind my back. With Dorothy sick, Poppy needs someone else in her life, and she gets on with you. But I don't want her disappointed, and that's all the church has in store for her."

Confusion scattered her thoughts. "I don't understand. You want me to stay?"

"You saw how well things worked out with Ms. Whiting, the nanny. I don't have anyone else I trust to watch out for Poppy," he admitted. "I can't spare anyone from the main office. More importantly,

Poppy doesn't know the people there as well as she does you."

"I haven't been here all that long." Tessa wasn't sure why she was objecting. She wanted nothing more than to stay, to be part of this family.

"You're determined to sink your own ship, aren't you?" Looking perplexed, he shook his head. "It's not the length of time, but I guess what people call the quality of it. Poppy took to you the first day. She doesn't do that with everybody. She's good-spirited and friendly, but not open to strangers. Probably because I discourage her from it." His eyes took on a faraway look, then he pushed back thick hair. "Why don't you forget about work for now? I have to study the surveys. I'll do that and we can get back together this afternoon. You can take Poppy to church. It'll save Cindy a trip."

Tessa hesitated. "I don't mind working."

"But you do mind missing church."

She couldn't lie about that, so she remained silent.

"Just as I thought. You might want to help Poppy pick out what to wear. I wasn't...very helpful when I was upstairs."

"Thank you, Morgan. And I'm sorry I resorted to subterfuge."

"At least your motives were good," he conceded.

Feeling like an olive that had gone through a dozen presses, she nodded. Among worry, lack of sleep and stress, she felt suddenly weary. Watching Morgan leave, she sank back into her chair. She'd just offered her resignation. And that would have meant losing her housing as well as her income. But her only thoughts had been how she'd feel leaving Poppy and Morgan behind.

How had she let her feelings become so entangled?

Glancing at the clock, Tessa realized she needed to get moving so that she and Poppy would be ready in time. First she called Cindy, then she headed upstairs, not seeing Morgan. He was probably in the dining room, she guessed.

Poppy's door stood ajar. Still, Tessa knocked lightly.

"Hi!" Poppy greeted her. "I'm going to sunny school!"

"I heard. Why don't we pick something real pretty to wear?"

Chapter Eleven

By three o'clock that afternoon, Morgan was more than ready for Tessa to get to work. He had a portfolio filled with surveys and well logs. Although Harper was an oil transportation company, that didn't preclude him from seeking oil leases or participating in new wells drilled on promising sites. His advantage was in securing leases before competitors caught wind of his plans. He saw it as putting more eggs in his collective basket of business. And he came by it naturally. His great-grandfather had been a lease hound, always one step ahead of his competitors.

Checking his watch, he hoped Tessa would hurry back from her cottage, where she'd gone to change clothes and eat lunch after church. Poppy had regaled him with an account of Sunday school and junior church all through their lunch. Unfortunately, she'd also begged to see Dorothy. But not yet, he decided regretfully. All the machines and tubes she was hooked up to would frighten Poppy. And Dorothy couldn't yet speak. Thinking of the woman almost as close to him as his own mother, Morgan swallowed. What if she never fully recovered?

A light knock sounded at the study's double doors. Looking up, he knew before seeing her that it was Tessa. She carried a tray with a carafe of coffee and two mugs. "Nancy insisted on making us a pot of coffee. Said we couldn't work without one."

He nodded, trying not to be annoyed by the delay. Even though he had been the one to send Tessa off to church that morning, he had hoped to have made quite a bit of progress by midafternoon. But lunch had stretched out longer than he expected.

"Nancy also said that she won't normally be working on Sundays," Tessa continued as she made a place for the tray on the desk. "That she's come in these last Sundays because of Dorothy taking ill so quickly." Tessa put just the right amount of sugar in one mug, cream in the other, poured the coffee and passed him a mug. She pulled open the wooden shelf on her side of the desk. Resembling a cutting board, it gave her a work space of her own while sitting at the desk. A tablet computer slid out of the space.

Morgan pulled up the first survey and began to discuss the specifics. Tessa kept up with him, searching her computer to verify each tract.

Two hours passed and Morgan glanced at his watch.

"What is it?" Tessa asked, seeing the motion.

"I have to get these to Houston tonight. The meeting's first thing in the morning."

Tessa frowned. "I don't have a meeting on your schedule for tomorrow."

"No, this one's for the geologists and engineers."

"Couldn't someone else from the office deliver them?" she asked, no doubt remembering the one packet he'd allowed Sherry to deliver. He frowned, still wishing Janet had ferried it herself instead of trusting her assistant.

"I'm short on staff, at least on Sundays. And these surveys are confidential. I can't trust them to a courier. Frankly, I don't want to trust them to anyone."

Poppy pushed open the office door, rushing toward her father. "We forgot!"

Confused, he glanced at her expectant face. "What did we forget?"

"Cornflake!" she exclaimed. "You said we could take him out every week. And we didn't yet."

"Ah, sweetheart, I have to go to Houston."

Her face fell.

"We just took Cornflake out last Saturday." The ride wasn't one he'd quickly forget.

"But not *this* Saturday," Poppy protested.

"It's work," he explained as her features began to crumble. "I'm sorry."

"I could go," Tessa offered. "To Houston, I mean. I'm guessing the building has twenty-four-hour security?"

He nodded reluctantly.

"A phone call from you and I can get in the office."

"You're not familiar with the place—"

"Do you have a secured spot for the envelope?"

Morgan hesitated. He had a small suite of offices in Houston that operated with a minimal staff. "In my office." Besides himself, only Janet had a key.

"Draw a diagram and I'll find it."

"Yes!" Poppy chimed in. "Please, Daddy?"

"Unless trust is the issue," Tessa added quietly.

He wasn't going to rise to that. "The quarters in the city are small. Finding my office won't be a problem, but I do keep it locked," he responded, hating to see the disappointment in Poppy's face.

"Then I'm guessing you have the key," Tessa replied.

"So I can ride Cornflake?" Poppy asked, bouncing up and down.

Knowing he was beaten, Morgan smiled at his daughter. He didn't want Tessa to keep taking on more duties. She must have put in a hundred hours this week alone. But he couldn't deny how happy she was making Poppy. Mentally sketching a few calculations, he frowned. "It'll be late by the time you'd be driving back."

She shrugged, seemingly unfazed. "Won't bother me."

"It would bother *me*. Before you leave, make a hotel reservation. If you can't get one, the trip's off for you."

"I'll stay with my parents."

"A bit last-minute," he protested.

"That won't bother my parents," she replied.

The entire trip bothered Morgan, but another glance at Poppy's excited expression kept him from insisting on making the run to Houston himself.

Since she knew the route well, Tessa's drive to Houston passed quickly enough. Once downtown, she located the building easily. Street after street of skyscrapers intimidated some, but not her. She loved the energy of the city, the promise of dazzling deals being conducted in boardrooms, the blur of so many thoughts and ideas. Relishing the city buzz, she used to walk from her office to stores, restaurants, the massive downtown library. Glancing around, she inhaled the humid air shunted by a subtle breeze.

More Fortune 500 companies were headquartered there than any other city besides New York. The possibilities were exhilarating.

She missed a lot about Houston. But not the memories. Even now, she crossed her arms against any intrusion. Not that it did any good. The emotions invaded her thoughts. Karl still peppered not only her memory, but all the places they'd shared, the streets she now walked on.

Smile dimming, she pushed through the revolving door fronting the building she sought. A sole security guard manned the reception desk.

She took out her driver's license and showed it to him. He took a photocopy of her ID, then instructed her to sign in. "When you're ready to leave, sign out here."

"Thank you."

Leaving him, she ventured to the towering elevator banks. She pushed the up button on one that said it would go to the thirtieth floor, about halfway to the top.

It was quiet in the lobby, even quieter in the elevator despite the soft whoosh lifting her high into the building. Just as Morgan had described, Harper's offices were tucked into one corner of the thirtieth floor.

She used Morgan's electronic card to gain entry into the reception area. The door shut behind her, a loud echo in the silence. Empty commercial buildings had always spooked her a bit. In the years she'd worked, she was never alone in an office. Other colleagues were always plugging away late into the evening, as well. It hit her how different this felt from the office in Morgan's home. It didn't bother her to be alone there.

Glancing around, she spotted the individual offices Morgan had described. His was, appropriately, the corner office. But the small bank of offices would all have view windows, she realized. The interior had been configured to take advantage of the space. Nice.

She reached inside her purse for the key to Morgan's office. Pausing, she studied the other offices.

Why didn't Morgan fill them with people who could share the burden of management?

Taking a step forward, she noticed a strip of light beneath Morgan's office door. That odd trace of fear emerged. "You're being ridiculous," she admonished herself in a whisper. "And you're whispering." But she wasn't lightened by the reminder. "The light probably got left on Friday," she told herself determinedly.

Her hand shook as she fitted the key in the door. "Quit being so silly!" The lock turned and she pushed in the door.

Seeing a figure bent over the desk, she couldn't withhold a tiny shriek.

She received a louder shriek in return.

"Tessa?" Janet Divo exclaimed, her hands flying to her chest. "What are you doing here?" She exhaled, her breath still short. "You scared the life out of me." She raised one arm, smoothing back already perfect blond hair.

Tessa finally smiled. "I hate to admit it but empty offices give me the creeps."

"Me, too. And I didn't hear the outside door open." Her face took on a quizzical expression. "Why are you here?"

"Just an errand for Morgan."

Janet laughed. "Glad you're not the bogeyman."

"You, too."

Still smiling, Janet straightened up a file folder and tamped the pages in place. "Anyway, welcome to our office! I haven't made any coffee but it'll only take a few minutes to brew a pot, if you'd like a cup."

"Not for me," Tessa replied. "I'm not staying."

"Going back to Rosewood tonight, then?"

"No. I'm going to spend the night with my parents. They live in Magnolia. It's last-minute, but they don't mind. I suspect we'll stay up too late talking and defeat the purpose of staying over, but I haven't been home to visit since I moved."

"It has been busy," Janet concurred. "Hopefully, you'll make it to the main office in Rosewood soon."

"I keep thinking that, too." So far there'd been no need to go to the corporate offices, and with Poppy in her charge, it wasn't practical. She had passed the three-story building on Main Street that housed Harper Petroleum once, but she had been heading to the stationery store on an errand, Poppy in tow.

Janet thumped her forehead. "I'm sorry. Can I help you find something?"

Uncomfortably, Tessa remembered that Morgan had said the package was confidential. Of course, Janet had a key to this private office, so she must be trustworthy. "Not really. Just an envelope to drop off."

Janet raised her eyebrows. "And Morgan had you drive into the city for that?"

Still not comfortable discussing the confidential errand, Tessa shrugged. "Just needed to get it here, and Morgan's spending time with Poppy, riding horses, so I volunteered."

"That was good of you."

Tessa deflected the praise. "Gives me a chance to see my parents, so it's a win-win." Not knowing how long Janet would be there, Tessa realized she couldn't outstay the other woman. Crossing the room, she opened one of the bottom drawers of the desk and slid the package inside. "Morgan will look for it here."

Janet nodded.

Knowing she didn't have an excuse to linger, Tessa smiled. "I'd better be going. My parents are holding dinner for me."

"Have a good visit," Janet replied.

"Thanks. I will." Departing, she had the uneasy sensation that she was leaving the place unguarded, unprotected. Silly. Janet was there. Why didn't that make her feel better?

Magnolia was outside Houston's city limits. Once completely rural, the area was now loaded with developments that encroached on the thickly wooded hamlet. When her parents had purchased the parcel of acreage, Houston had yet to grow out this far. But with time, the city had pushed past Tomball, then with the efficiency of army ants, had marched down the road, cloaking the small towns in its path with big-city traffic, stores and restaurants.

Her parents were getting itchy to move. Their dream had been to live in the country. A Houston suburb was not in their plans. Still, the house was lovely. Just what they'd envisioned. Although her mother, Sheila, said there were things she would change if she could build again.

Tessa turned into the long driveway that led to an oversize garage, past the barn and pond. Both were her father's pet projects. He collected antique tools and signs, and the barn had been built more for design than function. But the pond was thriving with fish that the state stocked at no cost. The program had been established to keep native species dominant.

"There you are!" her dad greeted her with a huge hug. "Not a minute too soon."

"Sorry I'm so late," she greeted him. "Took a little longer to drive in than I thought."

"Traffic," he responded. "It's everywhere. Can't outrun it anymore."

"It was bumper-to-bumper near downtown," she admitted. "Commuters and travelers, I suppose."

"Well, I'm glad you're out of that office building," her mother said as she joined them, hugging Tessa, then encircling her waist with one arm. "Never liked being in one alone." She shook in mock fear.

"Must be genetic," Tessa surmised. "It's as though the life of the building leaves with the workforce and then it's kind of shadowy in the night."

Sheila shivered. "Youch. I'm even gladder that you're out of it. I made enchiladas." Her favorite.

"You didn't have to go to so much trouble, Mom."

"I'd like to see you try to stop her," Edward said

drily. "And there's a death-by-chocolate cake hidden in the kitchen for dessert."

"Edward! That was supposed to be a surprise."

He didn't blink. "Surprise!"

Tessa laughed. Her parents had that effect on her. Always optimistic and open, they had been fun parents. Not that they let her run wild, just that they shared everything with her. Her mother had been thirty-six when Tessa was born and both her parents had prayed for a child. They had been married nine years when she made her appearance. A blessing, they often declared, a gift from heaven.

Tessa walked with them toward the kitchen. "Sorry this was so last-minute."

"We'll take what we can get," her father replied. "Now, tell us about Rosewood and why it's so much better than Houston."

Tessa did her best to describe the charming small town with old-fashioned values and a caring community.

"I like the sound of keeping superstores and chains out," Edward remarked. "Very sensible. When you have something worth preserving, it's great to know people are."

"Cindy always told me what a wonderful place Rosewood is, but I thought that had more to do with Flynn than the town. But it is unique. Instead of a shuttered Main Street, the local businesses are thriving. Most of the owners are descendants of the town founders."

"Wow," her mother summed up.

"Exactly. And not one T-shirt shop," Tessa added. "It's like something you'd see on a postcard."

"How about your job?" Edward questioned. "Is it postcard perfect, as well?"

"It's good," she replied truthfully. "Different than I expected."

"How so?" her mother asked.

Tessa explained Poppy's situation, then Dorothy's stroke. "So my job sort of converged—I'm half assistant and half nanny."

"And you like that?" Edward asked.

She nodded. "Poppy's a delight. Morgan works hard but that just makes me admire him more. Doesn't make me resent my workload."

Her parents exchanged a glance.

"What's that about?" Tessa questioned. "The look?"

"Sounds like you really like your boss," Sheila replied.

Tessa caught their train of thought and flipped the kill switch. "No, it's nothing like that. He's a widower."

"I hear they can remarry," Sheila said tartly.

"Only to someone who wants to get married," Tessa reminded them. "I've sworn that off."

"One bad apple—"

"I couldn't tell a bad apple before. What makes you think I'd want to try fishing in that bushel again?"

"This Morgan doesn't sound like a bad apple."

"No. And in a way he's like me—off of romance. He's still completely in love with his wife."

"Of course," Sheila replied calmly.

"Then why—"

"Would you want someone you loved to stop caring about your memory? To *get over* loving you and losing you?" Sheila smiled gently. "A good man has enough love to devote some to the memory of his wife and the rest to a new love."

"I never thought about it that way," Tessa admitted. "But there's nothing between us." She thought of their shared moments in the moonlight, the soft sighs of the night, the loneliness when Morgan was gone.

"That's not to say there won't be something between you in the future," Sheila rebutted. "Life's like that. You always wanted to package up life in perfect increments, but it doesn't work that way. Sounds like you might have met another compartmentalist. He probably doesn't know he is one any more than you do."

"Gee, thanks," Tessa muttered.

Sheila rubbed Tessa's shoulders. "Well, now that we've roasted you, how 'bout we see to dinner?"

"Tessa and enchiladas," Edward said gleefully. "Doesn't get better than that."

Tessa smiled but her mother's words played a game of tag in her thoughts. She had to be wrong. Morgan Harper was a self-contained, reserved, completely private man. Just because they shared office space and occasionally a twilight walk didn't mean… Tessa swallowed.

Karl popped into her thoughts like a barbed dagger. She had shared plenty of walks with him before they'd married and afterward. In that time she had never guessed the truth of his heart. Nor his ability to switch off their marriage like a bad connection. She couldn't…she wouldn't go through that again. Not that Morgan was open to any of those feelings. His love for his late wife was like a cloak that fitted him to perfection. An armor that enabled him to parent Poppy and deal with life. Her parents were sweet, but they'd have better luck matchmaking with a dwarf and a giant. And the outcome would be far prettier.

Chapter Twelve

Morgan expected Tessa to be gone all morning since she'd stayed the night with her parents. He was surprised when she trotted into the office just before nine o'clock.

"Sorry I'm late," she greeted him. "My mother insisted on feeding me before I left. And not something simple. How was the ride yesterday?"

He thought of Poppy's joy and softened. "It's not going to be easy to say no in the future."

Tessa tilted her head. "That's good, isn't it?"

In a perfect world. One that made no additional demands on his time. "Any problems getting into the office yesterday?"

She didn't blink at the sudden change of topic. "No. Security was expecting me. The keys worked. Went well."

"Anything out of the ordi—"

"Tessa!" Poppy hollered, running into the room at top speed. "I got to ride Cornflake! And we had ice cream!"

"Wow! You scored, huh?"

"Uh-huh." She bounded across the room to hang on Tessa's arm. "Did you bring me anything?"

"Poppy!" Morgan chided.

"It's okay." Tessa reached into her jacket pocket, withdrawing a small turquoise hair bow. "My mother made this for you." She glanced up at Morgan. "She likes crafts and I told her about how much Poppy enjoyed shopping for hair bows, but that we couldn't find a turquoise one. Blue *or* green, yes, but not turquoise. My mother has ribbon in every color imaginable. Her craft room is huge."

"She's nice," Poppy declared.

Tessa chuckled. "You'll have to meet her."

"When?"

"Well, when they come to visit," Tessa replied.

"When's that?"

Tessa met Morgan's eyes and he shrugged a fraction to indicate the visit and its timing was up to her. Tessa didn't immediately look away. Despite his resolve, something stirred within him.

"We'll have to see," Tessa replied.

"When Dorothy comes home?" Poppy asked innocently.

Tessa cleared her throat, her voice husky. "That sounds good."

Morgan kept his gaze on Tessa, still wondering at the effect she had on him.

"Doesn't it?" Tessa prodded gently.

What?

"It'll be good when Dorothy's well enough to come home," she told him, helping him get back on track with the conversation.

Her effort was necessary, vital even. He cleared his throat. "Yes, it will." He forced his thoughts away from the woman who stood in front of him. Refocusing, he thought of Dorothy, how he had hoped that she would recuperate at a faster pace. Knowing her, he guessed that she would improve more once she was at home. He hoped that time was coming sooner rather than later.

Glancing away from Tessa, he checked his watch and realized that he had time to stop at the hospital before his first meeting. If things worked out, he hoped to let Poppy visit in a day or so. He and Alvin had discussed the idea and both believed a visit would be good for Dorothy.

He was grateful for the progress Dorothy had made. Even if she never regained her complete mobility, the immediate fear of losing her was now greatly diminished. It had been such a relief, Morgan acknowledged, remembering his brief visit earlier.

Pleased to see the light in her eyes, Morgan had clasped Dorothy's hand. "You're feeling a little better."

She nodded, a small, uncertain motion.

"Alvin tells me your work with the speech therapist is going well."

She struggled until one word emerged. "Poppy?"

He gently squeezed her hand. "She's fine, but she

misses you. We all do. Tessa's spending time with her. And she's surprisingly good with her. Tessa was so stiff when she first got to Rosewood. Not so much anymore."

Dorothy weakly pressed his hand.

A knot of emotion formed in his throat. "It'll be so good when you come home. I sure miss you."

Although one side of her face didn't cooperate, she managed a lopsided smile and love settled in her eyes.

"Alvin," she struggled again, forcing out the name.

"I'm doing my best, but he's determined to stay glued to your side until you come home."

Dorothy managed a small half smile.

"Soon," Morgan promised. "Soon."

"What do you want to start with?" Tessa asked, breaking into his thoughts.

Morgan scrambled to regroup. At the top of the list, he realized Tessa needed some time of her own after the late run to the city, then her early start that morning. Which meant he couldn't visit Dorothy. "Nothing. You're taking some time off."

"It's not necessary."

"I didn't expect you back this early. Go, enjoy yourself."

"I have been wanting to visit the Children's Home," Tessa admitted. "I just went the one time with Cindy. I think Poppy would have a good time, if it's all right for me to bring her."

He wondered at what she considered leisure time. "I meant for *you* to have some time." Morgan glanced at his daughter.

"I will be," Tessa insisted. "I think Poppy would enjoy meeting the kids. And we could stop at Maddie's Tea Cart first. Cindy says they have kid-friendly drinks."

Morgan's brow furrowed. "I really think you need some time off to yourself, without Poppy in tow."

"It's better for me when Poppy comes along." She met his eyes again, evoking, enticing. "I enjoy her so much."

Fending off the thoughts her eyes were causing, he cleared his throat, but not his mind. So he tried to concentrate on his daughter. "Even so, I'm sure you need your own space without any demands on your time."

"She's not a demand," Tessa replied quietly.

Morgan couldn't fight that sentiment. Sure, he was prejudiced, but Poppy was an endearing child. Still, he didn't imagine that every single moment with her was a joy to anyone other than himself.

"If you're sure…"

"Yay!" Poppy jumped up and down. "Can I wear my blue-green dress? The one the new bow matches. Please?"

Morgan automatically turned to Tessa since he didn't know what girls and women wore to tea.

"I could wear my turquoise dress, too," Tessa contemplated aloud.

Tessa and Poppy strolled out toward the entry hall, totally wrapped up in their conversation. Strangely, he didn't feel left out. Instead it seemed right that Poppy had a woman to watch over the girlie things he was inept with. Laughter spilled down the staircase as they climbed. If he was smart, he'd leave before Tessa changed into the dress that would bring her eyes to the color of an ocean lagoon.

Tessa held Poppy's hand as they stood at the front door of the Children's Home. They'd already had tea. Poppy had gamely tried the quiche, something she hadn't eaten before. And she was excited to visit the home and meet some of the kids.

Entering, Poppy recognized a few children her own age whom she'd met in Sunday school. Going from uncertain to unabashedly smiling, Poppy was engulfed by a small group of kids.

"I didn't know you were going to be here," Cindy exclaimed, walking out of the kitchen.

"It's kind of impromptu," Tessa explained. "Morgan gave me the morning off and so we had tea at Maddie's and thought it would be fun to stop by. Since most of the older kids are in school, maybe Poppy can play with the ones closer to her age."

"Looks like that's already happening." Cindy smiled as the kids giggled and drew Poppy into their game. Each child was pretending to be an animal. Poppy happily chose to be a horse.

"So why did Morgan give you the morning off?"

Tessa briefly explained the trip to the city. "He thought I'd want my own space," she quoted. "Not sure why."

Cindy's smile softened. "So that's how it is."

Frowning, Tessa drew her eyebrows together.

"Spoken with love," Cindy assured her. "You've all gotten so much closer. I was afraid for a while that Morgan would chase you away, but I don't think I need to worry about that any longer."

"You're erecting mountains in molehill territory," Tessa said, dismissing her friend's conclusions.

"If you could see what I see," Cindy murmured. "Then again, perhaps it's best not to just yet."

Tessa shook her head but Cindy continued smiling. And nodding. And looking as though she'd just struck gold.

Leaving early didn't save him. When Morgan returned, Tessa and Poppy still wore their blue-green frocks. He looked everywhere except at Tessa's eyes, certain what they would contain.

Hours later, dinner eaten, bath taken, Poppy was ready for bed. As had become her new habit, Tessa knelt beside the girl to listen to her recite her nightly prayers. So far Morgan hadn't put a stop to the practice. Poppy prayed for all those she knew, sometimes including Cornflake.

"Bless Daddy, Alvin and Dorothy. Please make Dorothy all better. And bless Tessa, and make Daddy be home more," Poppy concluded.

Each sweet, innocent thought resonated with Tessa. Climbing into bed, Poppy reached for Freckles, pulling the stuffed dog close.

Tessa flipped off the overhead light, leaving the lamp on. Its base would remain lit as a night-light once the lamp was turned off. Drawing up the blanket, she tucked it in securely. "Snug as a bug in a rug."

Poppy giggled. "You say that every time."

Smiling, Tessa nodded. "My mother said that to me every time she tucked me in."

"Can I have a story and a song?"

"I think we can manage that." Tessa picked up a book that held several stories. Knowing Poppy's favorite, *Cinderella*, she flipped to it and read about the fabled princess. Then Tessa sang a quiet rendition of "Over the Rainbow."

Contented, Poppy snuggled deeper into her pillow. Tessa switched off the lamp, allowing only the soft night-light portion to stay lit. "Good night, Poppy."

"Night," Poppy replied, her voice sounding a bit sleepy.

Tessa glanced into the hallway and thought she saw the shadows move. She shook off the thought, certain she was just tired herself. Leaving Poppy's door ajar, she walked downstairs and into the kitchen to make a cup of tea.

"Hey," Morgan greeted Tessa as she entered the kitchen.

"I didn't know you were home," Tessa replied. "I

could have kept Poppy up long enough for you to see her."

"I just got here. She was too tired to stay up any longer."

Tessa lifted her eyebrows. "How did you know?"

"Girls' day out," he improvised. "Bound to make her tired."

"True. I barely left her room."

And he'd barely beaten her to the kitchen by using the back stairs.

"Would you like a cup?" Tessa asked.

Baffled, he didn't reply.

"Of tea?" she added, holding up a cup.

"Uh, yeah. That'd be fine." His thoughts were crowded. He couldn't get the image of Tessa and Poppy out of his head. There was such a sweetness in the way she interacted with his daughter.

Tessa filled the electric teakettle and set it on the charger. "I'm having chamomile. That okay with you?"

"Fine." He'd never been much of a tea drinker. The kitchen wasn't quite right without Dorothy in it, but somehow Tessa made it seem cozy. He'd sat in the room late in the night when he couldn't sleep, but as he did everywhere, he always felt alone. Tessa had changed that.

It took only a few minutes for the electric kettle to reach a boil. Tessa brought over the cups, joining him at the table.

"I put in a drop of honey," she began. "Not enough for a sugar jolt."

The steaming cup smelled of herbs. "I'm not picky."

She laughed, then coughed to cover the sound.

"What?" he asked. "Something funny?"

"Well...don't take this wrong, but you could be considered picky."

"Why?"

She met his gaze, hers looking dubious. "Just that you're very particular."

"If a job's worth doing—"

"It's worth doing right," she finished for him. "I know."

"Something wrong with that?"

"Of course not. But you seem to live and breathe Harper Petroleum." She shrugged. "Just an observation."

"Then you won't mind me observing that you're a dyed-in-the-wool career woman."

She blanched. "You're right, of course."

He hated how she tensed up, then kept her gaze on her tea. "I didn't mean that negatively. You started at the bottom and worked your way up. I admire that. I had an *in* for my job." He made his tone persuasive, regretting the impulse to give back tit for tat.

She glanced up briefly. "It's not my place to question how you spend your time."

Her place had more than changed since he'd hired her—it was upside down. She should be all about business, but now she had burrowed her way into his personal life on every level. "Someone has to," he admitted, "and Dorothy's not here to do it."

A tiny smile flitted on her lips.

"So is that someone going to be you?" he asked, idly running his thumb around the rim of the cup, feeling its warmth, sensing hers so very close to him.

"I don't think anyone can fill Dorothy's shoes," Tessa replied, her breathing short.

No, but Tessa was evoking something else, something he hadn't felt since Lucy died. Startled by the thought, he jerked back his hand, overturning the cup.

Tessa grabbed a napkin, blotting up the spilled tea.

"Sorry, let me get that." He reached for the napkin but caught her hand instead.

She froze.

Her hand was soft beneath his, and it took him a few moments to release it. All of the day's postponed tensions spilled out.

"I can—"

"It'll just—" They both spoke at once, then fell silent.

Feeling more than a little ridiculous, Morgan drew back. "I'll grab a towel."

She studied the table as though it contained a Renaissance masterpiece. "Okay."

It took only seconds to wipe up the remaining tea.

"Would you like more?" she asked, looking first hopeful, then fearful.

"Well, I—"

She jumped up from her chair. "It'll take almost no time to make another cup. I don't normally use tea bags, but at night it's easier to fix chamomile that way. I love loose tea, but you need a really fine mesh strainer. Of course, the English consider our tea bags to be dust bags. And sometimes they are. The water's still hot in the kettle. One of the great things about electric kettles. And even if the water cools down, it reheats really fast."

Morgan didn't believe he'd heard her talk that much all at once since he met her. "Fine."

"Was the honey okay?"

"I didn't really get a chance to taste it," he reminded her.

She flushed, seeming to have trouble finding a resting spot for her hands. "Silly. I knew that." She finally stuck her hands into her pockets. The tea-kettle clicked, indicating the water had reached the boiling point. Tessa busied herself making the tea.

"Yours is getting cold," he said, accepting the fresh cup of tea.

"It's fine," she replied, waving away his concern. "I'm used to it. I get distracted a lot when I'm sipping tea. I'll be reading and forget about it. When I remember my tea, it has gone stone-cold."

He wondered what she read. And how many of her hours were spent that way. How any of her private hours were spent. "What are you reading now?"

"A historical novel," she replied.

"That your favorite genre?"

"I don't know." She still seemed nervous. "I'm not sure I really have a favorite. I read all kinds of books. Nothing's better than finding a new one to love."

A new one to love? The concept echoed in his thoughts, brought a physical pain. He wasn't ready to think about any sort of new love. The headache that stress brought on now pounded like a rock-hard fist. "If you don't mind, I'll take my tea upstairs," Morgan told her as he pushed back his chair, hearing the scrape of its legs against the wood floor.

"Oh, um, sure," she replied, looking surprised.

He didn't wonder at her surprise. He wasn't the slippers-and-tea type and he was pretty sure she knew it. Heading upstairs, he paused in front of Poppy's room to peek in on her, make certain she was sleeping all right.

As he did, Morgan couldn't force away the image of Poppy and Tessa just a short time earlier. Or the sweetness it evoked.

Chapter Thirteen

Poppy took tiny steps as she entered Dorothy's hospital room. She'd been a whirlwind of energy on the ride over. But the quiet room and banks of scary equipment seemed to sober her.

She reached for the closest adult—Tessa—and grabbed hold of her hand.

Tessa didn't mind. She knew Poppy was scared. Glancing at Morgan, she wondered how he was faring. He was the only one of them who had visited Dorothy, knew what to expect.

Quiet reigned. Dorothy was still connected to several machines that monitored her condition.

Not sure how Dorothy would look, Tessa squeezed Poppy's hand. As they approached the bed, she could tell the moment Dorothy spotted her favorite little girl.

Eyes bright, tears forming, she lifted the one hand that worked.

"It's okay," Tessa said quietly as she bent close to Poppy's ear.

Poppy rushed toward Dorothy, then paused when she saw that the tubes were attached.

Dorothy held out her good arm and Poppy's reluctance vanished as she accepted the hug.

"Are you almost all better?" Poppy asked when they finally parted.

Dorothy nodded.

And Tessa remembered that Morgan had told them Dorothy's voice was slow in returning.

"Hi, Alvin," Tessa greeted him. He looked older, drawn. No doubt he was exhausted. "It's good to see you."

Despite his fatigue, Alvin smiled. "You're all a sight for sore eyes."

"You, too," she responded sincerely.

Morgan set a bag with fresh clothes on the side table, then placed a box on the tray. "Stopped by the bakery. Fresh apple fritters and cherry kolaches. Got cheese for you, Dorothy." The kolaches, a regional favorite, were a Czech creation that had come with the pioneers from that country. The filling in the cheese variety tasted much like that of a cheese Danish. "I know Dorothy doesn't approve of store-bought pastries, but until she's ready to bake we'll have to make do."

One side of Dorothy's mouth edged up slightly. A smile, Tessa recognized. The realization warmed her heart. Studying Morgan, she noted that he was checking Dorothy's progress, as well. It touched her that this fiercely independent industry leader was as concerned over his housekeeper as a major deal in the making.

He boosted Poppy up onto the side of the bed. Dorothy's working side, Tessa realized. Stepping back, he brushed into Tessa. She started to move away, give them more space, some privacy. But Morgan caught her arm, stilling the action.

Swallowing, Tessa was terribly aware of him as they stood side by side while Poppy told Dorothy all about riding Cornflake and buying barrettes and hair bows.

Tessa was barely aware of what was being said as the tension from the night before accelerated. Her throat dried so rapidly she hoped she wouldn't have to speak. It would be a struggle not to croak when she did.

"I have a surprise," Poppy confided.

Dorothy's eyes widened.

Tessa stepped forward, handing the small gift bag to Poppy.

"Do you want me to open it?" Poppy asked, incredibly perceptive for a four-year-old.

Dorothy nodded.

Poppy pulled out the necklace they'd bought. "See, it has butterflies."

Dorothy's eyes brightened with a sheen of tears.

"Now, that's awful pretty," Alvin told her.

Tessa thought it was sweet that Alvin was so tuned in, knowing when to let Poppy's interaction play out and also when Dorothy needed a little assistance expressing what she couldn't quite manage to say.

Poppy studied the array of tubes and cords. "Maybe you could wear it when you come home."

That semismile of Dorothy's emerged as she nodded.

"But you can keep it here to look at," Poppy added.

Tessa had noticed all the fresh flowers in the room. One arrangement mimicked the one that sat on the round table in the foyer of Morgan's house. Well, Dorothy and Alvin's house, as well. A little bit of home in her hospital room, Tessa realized. They must have come from Morgan. She glanced at him again, wondering at all the sides of this unusual man. Could they all be genuine?

She thought of her parents' conviction that she and Morgan were of the same predilection. Silliness. Tessa and Morgan were as different as…well, Morgan and Karl. Her ex-husband would never have the sensitivity to keep a hospital room stocked with flowers to give it a homey feeling. Nor did he have the same dedication as Morgan. Oh, he liked making money and worked to make sure he did. But he didn't care about the fate of his coworkers. If a job came between him and a competitor, he had no qualms shooting down the other man. And then there was Poppy. For all that Karl wanted an heir, most children annoyed him. He thought they were noisy and sticky. It had never occurred to her what a dichotomy that was. She'd been tossed aside for being unable to have a baby, when in truth, Karl wasn't fond of them. But an heir was expected in his family.

"Dorothy, Alvin, we've enjoyed the visit but we better go now," Morgan was saying. "Give you some time together."

Tessa smiled at the pair as Poppy gave them each hugs. A dose of that sweetness should speed Dorothy's recovery. No longer somber, the room was brightened by Poppy's smiles and giggles.

"When you get all better, we can have a tea party," Poppy told Dorothy. "I'll make a cake."

Struggling, Dorothy strove to speak, her voice broken, weak. "I love you."

Poppy hugged her again. "I love you, too."

Alvin's eyes looked moist and Tessa didn't dare check Morgan's gaze or they'd all be bawling before they left. The power of those simple words had changed more lives than all the world's wars. Considering her past, that much power was downright terrifying.

Trees that were well over one hundred years old provided plentiful shade for games, picnic lunches and playing children. Squirrels fussed at each other, squabbling over acorns. Rosewood's city park hadn't changed much in the past century. Playground equipment had been updated, but not much else needed altering.

Feeling that these playdates were really good for Poppy, Tessa watched with Cindy as Poppy and

Cindy's youngest, Katy, played. The rest of Cindy's children were in school. Katy, who was three, had been named for Cindy's best friend, Katherine Carlson, the person who had inspired Cindy to move to Rosewood.

The girls played on the combination slide and monkey bars, and Poppy was proving to be quite the little mother, making sure the smaller child could climb the rungs, watching so she didn't fall.

"I'm pleased that Poppy's playing so well with Katy," Tessa admitted. "You know I've been worried that not having had much contact with other children might make her too domineering."

"Her Sunday school teacher told me she's a delight," Cindy replied. "Not that I'm surprised. Dorothy and Alvin are as down-to-earth as it comes. Morgan is, too. I did worry for a while that when he lost Lucy he might let Poppy get away with murder, but he seems to find the right balance."

Reluctantly, Tessa nodded.

"You don't think so?"

"Yes and no," Tessa replied. "He enforces rules, but he doesn't spend enough time with Poppy. He works seven days a week. I understand why. He carries the entire management load. But he could fix that problem if he'd just delegate. What point is there in preserving a company if it means he never sees his daughter?"

"I suppose at first when Lucy died, work was all

that kept him sane." Cindy waved at little Katy, who was climbing ahead of Poppy up to the slide.

"But he has good people," Tessa argued. "Ronnie Broussard in East Texas could carry that entire region. And just cutting down his trips there would give Morgan a lot more time for Poppy. Then here, there's Janet Divo."

Cindy lifted her eyebrows.

"What?" Tessa questioned.

Shaking her head, Cindy looked down into her cup of punch. "Nothing."

"Which is why you're trying to crawl into your cup. What is it?" Tessa insisted.

"You've probably already noticed," Cindy began.

"Nope."

"Years ago they went together in high school," Cindy began reluctantly. "Everyone thought they'd get married."

"Oh, I did hear about that. I was told it's ancient history."

"It is to Morgan," Cindy revealed. "But Janet…"

Tessa blinked in surprise. "She still cares for him?"

"Janet has a huge crush on Morgan, has ever since high school. When they went to different colleges, they just naturally grew apart. And once he met Lucy, well, that was it. He never gave Janet a second thought." Cindy fiddled with her cup. "Some people think she went to work at Harper just to be close to him."

"Any merit in that?"

Cindy shrugged. "I honestly don't know. But it's kind of odd. She has a degree in business and could probably do better than being an office manager, but she's stayed in the job for years. Morgan didn't consider promoting her to the position you took."

"Maybe she likes what she's doing."

"And she hasn't ever married."

"Because she hasn't met the right guy?" Tessa guessed.

"Possibly. But I really don't think she's looking." Cindy tilted her head as the sun highlighted her distinctive hair. "I don't ever see her with anyone at church or anywhere else. She lives alone. She did live with her parents, but they decided to move back to the Panhandle, where they're from."

"And she didn't go with them," Tessa mused, wondering why. What held a young woman to a town without family or a romantic interest? "Does she have other extended family here?"

"No. Her brother moved back to the Panhandle, too, when he inherited his uncle's ranch."

It was puzzling. Not that Rosewood lacked charm. But why choose a solitary life? The irony hit her and she sighed.

"What?" Cindy asked.

Tessa shook her head slowly. "I'm sitting here trying to understand why a single woman chooses to live in a town without family or a boyfriend. That describes me perfectly."

Cindy placed her hand over Tessa's. "You do have family. Me, us. We're family. I've never believed it was restricted to blood relatives. Maybe Janet has good friends who give her the same feeling."

"That or she's in love with Morgan."

"Whoo." Cindy's eyes grew rounder. "That was a leap."

"From crush to love?" Tessa put her cup on the redwood table. "Not if she's loved him all along." She hesitated, phrasing her next statement carefully. "Just because he was married doesn't mean she changed how she felt about him."

"Well, that's my life story," Cindy admitted. "I hadn't thought it out that clearly. I always felt like I was running away, whereas Janet remained here, stayed for all of it. But in the end it boils down to the same thing. She was in love with a married man with no hope that he would return her feelings. Lucy dying just made him cling tighter to her memory. And Janet was probably invisible to him the entire time."

"Do you know much about Sherry?" Tessa questioned. "Janet's assistant?"

"Not really. She pretty much stays to herself. But that could be because I meet most of my contacts at church, through Flynn's business or even at the Tea Cart." Cindy frowned. "It is kind of weird that we never run into her. Why do you ask?"

"No special reason. Just that when I was talking to the two of them, she kept going on about Morgan and Janet's high school romance, like she had a thorn in her paw."

"I honestly have no idea why. I don't think she's from here." Looking puzzled, Cindy rested her chin in one hand. "I wonder how she knows about their romance."

"Don't ask me. I'm the newcomer, remember?"

"Vividly. Don't assume that the gossip is true. And even if it is, clearly Morgan's had time to let Janet into his life romantically, if that was what he was looking for. He must not have wanted to."

Tessa's eyes widened. "Don't you think *that's* a big leap?"

"You've only been here for months and you're closer to Morgan than Janet and she's been pining for him since high school!"

"I still say she may just enjoy her job." Tessa tried to imagine Morgan and Janet as a couple, but the combination wouldn't process in her thoughts.

"You've never been deliberately obtuse," Cindy noted as she watched Katy.

"What?"

"Katy, let Poppy get on the slide," Cindy called out.

Distracted, Tessa checked on Poppy. The tot waved and a tide of warmth flooded her. Sensing motion behind her, Tessa swiveled, seeing a woman with two children approaching the table beside them. The young woman was heavily pregnant, walking somewhat slowly. The duo with her, boys who looked about a year apart, carried a small cooler.

Tessa's own infertility suddenly seemed incredibly stark, inescapable. Like a reopened wound, the pain attacked. Thinking the gash had been sutured, she didn't expect her heart to hurt this much. Would it always be like this? Would the sight of babies and pregnant women always turn her world black?

"Tessa," Cindy repeated, concern coloring her voice. "What's wrong?"

"Nothing." Tessa cleared her throat, but her own voice remained raspy. "Really. Nothing." She turned around, focusing on Poppy, who never triggered the pain. Instead she was a solace, a get-out-of-jail-free card. Tessa didn't know why, only that her connection with the child was grounded, real. She wasn't a concept or rationalization, she was simply loved. Blinking, she realized it was true. More than simple affection, she loved this child.

It was frightening to think if her job went awry, so would her connection to Poppy. Glancing back over her shoulder, she watched as the pregnant woman sighed and leaned against the picnic table. She would have to learn how to shut out the associations, she decided, the ones that caused so much distress.

And she didn't dare dwell on Cindy's theories. Because then she might believe that what she glimpsed in Morgan's eyes was the beginning of something new, something real.

Chapter Fourteen

A few days later, Morgan rechecked the bottom drawer of his desk. The survey was still there. Since he'd casually tossed it inside, he couldn't tell if it had been removed and then replaced.

He had spent the past eighteen months cultivating a relationship with the owner of that land. Certain that he could garner the oil leases on the petroleum-rich property, he was stunned to learn that the man signed with someone else—Traxton Energy. The umbrella company that owned Traxton Oil, the outfit Tessa had been with for a decade.

Morgan hated that the thought had popped immediately to mind. Mentally scanning through the past months, he tried to think of who else could have leaked the information. His office staff had been with him for years. They were completely trustworthy. Morgan frowned. Well, most of them had been with him a long time. There were the hires from Adair Petroleum's layoffs, but those people had even more reason to be loyal. He had rescued them when they were left jobless during a high-unemployment time.

He hadn't been able to hire everyone. That would have been impossible with the resources Harper had. But he'd felt the gratitude of those who joined Harper. However, none of those people had been in his home. Again he felt that twitch of missing Dorothy and Alvin. During their watch, the house had always seemed safe when he had to leave it. Now, it was far more uncertain. Nancy cooked the meals and Heather cleaned the house, but neither watched out for the place. That had fallen to Tessa when he wasn't there. She would know who their visitors had been.

Despite his shifting feelings, he hadn't fully realized how much he had come to count on her. She was taking care of Poppy and, with Janet's and Sherry's help, she was completing all her work. In addition, she had stepped in to supervise all the other things a household needed to function. Since he'd hired a small staff and lawn service, Morgan had not given it another thought, but Tessa had. They turned to Tessa for their instructions, not him.

Morgan pressed his forehead, recognizing the beginning of a headache. They had been far less frequent lately. Funny, he just noticed that.

At least he still had the prize site intact—the survey safely locked away in his Houston office. That one was his real find. Getting those leases would ensure a long life for Harper. He just had to wait until the current agreement expired. With all the cutbacks in exploration, the company holding the leases hadn't developed the untapped treasure. But Morgan's grandfather had held the adjacent leases back in the day, and that oil was still pumping.

His cell phone rang. Alvin.

"Morgan? Everything's okay here," Alvin began, not wanting to worry Morgan. "In fact, better than okay. They're going to move Dorothy to a rehab place tomorrow."

"What about her speech therapy?"

He envisioned Alvin nodding, then the older man spoke. "Yep. They have one on staff. Physical therapy, too. Everything she needs. Idea is to get her ready to come home."

"That will be great, Alvin." Morgan swiveled toward the large window in his office. "The place isn't the same without you and Dorothy. I want to stress again that you're not to worry about having someone to do the work. Even when you're back, I think we need to keep on these extra people. I had no idea how much work you and Dorothy were doing. She deserves to have someone to help with the chores. So do you. There are plenty of other things that are more important—stuff I can only count on you for."

"Something wrong, Morgan?"

His old friend knew him well, but he couldn't worry the older man, whose hands were full. "Just thinking how good it will be when you and Dorothy are back home. Things aren't the same without you."

"I thought Tessa was helping out a lot."

"She is," Morgan agreed, that fact itching in his thoughts. "But she isn't family."

Alvin was quiet.

"But that's nothing for you to worry about," Morgan assured him.

"She and Poppy still getting on like a house afire?" Alvin questioned.

Morgan chuckled despite his concerns. "Poppy has us all going. Now she has *playdates*."

"Do tell. We just had playing in my day."

"I think it's a female thing, Alvin. At least I hope so."

"Well, I'd better get back to Dorothy. She's pretty excited about this move."

"Tell her Poppy will be jumping up and down until she comes home. We all miss you." Morgan surprised himself with the admission, but knew he could implicitly trust Alvin.

"We miss being home," Alvin acknowledged.

Morgan stared at the phone once the connection was gone. He remembered how Tessa had stepped in when Dorothy had her stroke. He could convince himself that it was a handy way for her to gain his trust. But there was no way she could have anticipated the emergency. And somehow he felt that whoever had taken the information had planned their move well. It seemed unlikely they would count on luck.

The house phone rang. Glancing at the caller ID,

he saw that it was the main office. He picked up the phone before the second ring. Janet greeted him.

Mentally shifting gears, he settled back in his chair. "Tell me something good, Janet."

She paused, then related the details of a call he needed to handle personally. "I tried calling Tessa," Janet explained. "But I couldn't reach her."

"She's out with Poppy," he replied. "I suppose she forgot to forward her calls."

"I can do it from here," Janet offered.

The pain in his head increased. "That would be helpful. Anything else, Janet?"

Again, a slight hesitation. "No, that's it. Anything for me?"

"Not at the moment. I'll check with Tessa and let you know."

"Check with…?" She paused. "Ah, fine, Morgan."

As he clicked off the phone, he thought of his words. When Miss Ellis had been his assistant, he'd never had to check with her to know his workload. Of course, that was before Dorothy had a stroke, before all their lives were turned upside down. Still, it bothered him.

He heard a flurry of noise in the hall, able to discern Poppy's voice over the clatter of footfalls and the rustle of movements. She sounded happy. Happier than he could remember.

"Daddy!" she greeted him only moments later.

"Hey," he responded as she ran across the study. Ignoring the wealth of paperwork strewn across his desk, she jumped into his lap. Not that he minded. He loved the quick hug she gave him. The tiny knot in his stomach that he always ignored whenever she was out of his sight relaxed finally. The worry was never far away, the fear that something might happen to her. There was no valid reason for the fear, but there had been no reason to suspect Lucy would die so unexpectedly, either.

"Guess where we went," she began.

Before he could reply, she told him. "We went to Aunt Cindy's kids' house." Children's Home, he interpreted silently. "And we played and had cookies."

Glancing up, he caught the fondness in Tessa's eyes as she looked at Poppy. Then she realized he was watching and lifted her gaze. There was a peace in her expression that he'd never seen before. That and something else. Something he couldn't put a name to.

"The kids there are so lucky, Daddy."

"Lucky?" he questioned, not understanding.

"They have kids to play with all the time," Poppy announced, her smile bright.

Again Morgan glanced up, seeing a knowing look on Tessa's face.

"The older kids were in school," Tessa explained. "But the younger ones were there, a built-in group of playmates."

"It was so much fun," Poppy declared. "Aunt Cindy said I can come and play whenever I want. Do you want to come next time?"

Nonplussed, he wasn't sure how to answer.

"We'll have to see about your father's work schedule," Tessa replied for him. "But now, don't you have something?" She nodded toward the hall.

Poppy jumped down, then ran to the entry hall. In seconds she was back with a little cardboard box. "This is for you."

"We went to the Tea Cart," Tessa explained. "And Poppy said this was a favorite."

He opened the box to see a slice of carrot cake. "It is. This looks homemade."

"Maddie makes her own desserts," Tessa agreed. "But you probably know that."

"I'd forgotten," he admitted. "I don't get there much these days."

"We brought home quiche," Tessa added. "I know it's not a real guy kind of meal, but we brought enough for everyone. I thought Nancy, Heather and Frank might like something different."

"Frank?" Morgan questioned, wondering who that might be. Had she met someone here in Rosewood? He hated the lurch in his gut.

"Your yardman," she replied. "He isn't here every day but he's here now. I did get some sausage kolaches for anyone who doesn't like quiche."

He realized she was just being thoughtful. Something that came naturally to her. Still, he wondered at his reaction.

"We had trouble deciding on dessert," she continued. "Everything looked so good, it was hard to pick.

Poppy and I finally decided that everyone would probably enjoy cheesecake."

"But we got cookies, too," Poppy confided. "Because I like them."

Guilt pervaded him. Just minutes earlier he had suspected Tessa of sabotage. Hardly fit her. Yet he still couldn't think who had gotten access to his confidential information.

Tessa studied Morgan, wondering at the different reactions that played out across his expression. Suspicion? Had she really seen that? Relief? Why?

"I'd better get everything into the kitchen so Nancy knows she doesn't have to cook tonight. Unless you'd rather have something else?"

Silence.

"Morgan?"

He lifted his gaze. "What?"

"Do you want Nancy to cook something for dinner? Or will the quiche and kolaches be okay?"

"They're fine," he replied, looking distracted.

"Okay, then."

Nancy was delighted by the bounty of food. "I love anyone else's cooking."

"I can understand that. It's like my love/hate relationship with the computer. I'm usually on it most of the day for work, so I really have no desire to fire up my laptop in the evenings."

"Um, that cheesecake looks good."

"The sauce is on the side," Tessa explained. "I

got strawberry and also caramel. Cindy said they're both fabulous."

"The Tea Cart is great," Nancy agreed. "Original and delicious, hard to beat."

"I'd better check on that infernal computer," Tessa said, realizing the time. Morgan had instructed her to take the day off, but she needed to make sure nothing important was sitting in her email inbox.

Nancy smiled as she stowed the cheesecake in the refrigerator.

It didn't take long for Tessa to learn that nothing crucial had arrived in her email. The morning mail was still bundled in the center of her desk. A cursory look showed nothing unusual. There was a white linen envelope with no return address that was made out to her. Awfully nice stationery for an advertisement, she thought, running her thumb over the expensive paper. She slid her letter opener under the flap. Open, the envelope appeared empty. Tessa turned it upside down and shook it. Nothing fell out. Strange. She looked again at her name and the address, the only writing on the envelope. Typed. Neatly. Not on a label, but directly on the envelope. If it had been important, Tessa reasoned, it would have a return address. She tossed the envelope into her wastebasket.

"Tessa?" Poppy was asking from beside her. "Do you have work for me?"

"Let's see." Tessa glanced over the remainder of the mail. She really needed to examine it more closely. Her gaze landed on the linen envelope. "Here we go. I need this letter to get ready for the post office."

Poppy smiled. Grabbing markers, she settled into her corner behind Tessa's desk. "Where should it go to?"

"Hmm. How about Houston?" Tessa replied, falling into the imaginary game.

"Okay." Poppy scribbled industriously on the envelope, not yet knowing how to write anything more than her letters and name.

Tessa smiled to herself, loving Poppy's joy in the tiniest things.

"Do you want me to write a store list?" Poppy questioned, referring to the scribbles she made while "writing" down the list of groceries.

"That would be so much help," Tessa replied. "I'm lucky to have such a good helper."

Poppy concentrated on the envelope, covering nearly the entire back side.

Tessa did feel incredibly lucky. Knowing children weren't in her future, she felt as though the Lord had given her this time with Poppy as a gift. Unspoiled, full of love, she was a delight.

"Can I have another one?" Poppy asked, holding up the envelope.

Tessa reached into the stationery drawer and pulled out a company envelope. "Where are you sending this one?"

"To Dorothy," Poppy replied without hesitation. "She needs get betters so she can come home."

Yes, sweetness. Pure, caring sweetness.

Chapter Fifteen

The following Saturday, Morgan tried to tell himself that he'd agreed to Poppy's plan only to humor her, but the lure of a late-afternoon ride had been impossible to resist. He also tried to tell himself that his acquiescence had nothing to do with Tessa, the fact that she had agreed to join them.

Although the sun was dipping toward the horizon, it still gave off enough bright beams to light up Tessa's silhouette. As she rode just ahead of him, with Poppy at her side, he watched the light catch her dark hair, linger over her profile. He didn't need to look to know that when the sunlight surrounded Tessa her eyes darkened to a Caribbean-toned aquamarine.

She and Poppy laughed over something. He wasn't paying attention to the words. He liked that Tessa laughed more now. She'd been so buttoned-up when he'd first met her. As unyielding as steel. Now she was more like a supple start of a willow tree.

Tessa turned around just then. He sucked in his breath. Logically, he'd always known she was pretty, but with the late-afternoon glow of the sun framing her face, he realized just how much.

"Going to join us?" she asked with a smile.

Clearing his throat, Morgan tried for casual. "Thinking I would."

Since he knew the layout of the land, he was usually the one to lead their little group. Clicking his tongue, he nudged his mount with his knees, riding forward.

Since he'd learned of Tessa's fear of heights, they had avoided winding up the hills. Instead he led them toward the arroyo. With clear weather, he didn't have to worry about flash floods. The dry creek bed was gently sloped, not so much as to trigger Tessa's fear of heights.

"Can we see flowers?" Poppy asked.

Knowing she meant wildflowers in the fields, he agreed. "Sure. You can pick a bouquet for Dorothy."

"For when we go see her," Poppy agreed happily.

Riding just a short distance, they spotted the scattered wildflowers that looked as though they'd been planned by one majestic hand to scatter over and between the wild grasses. Paintbrushes, with their bright orange blooms, wove between Indian blankets, purple verbena and deep rose wine cups. Bluebonnets seemed to bring the sky to the earth, a glorious union.

Tessa sighed when they reached the edge of the meadow. "It's amazing." Sitting up in her saddle, she twisted to take a better look around. "Flowers everywhere."

"Some people seem to have the idea that we only have bluebonnets growing wild. All these other flowers are just as pretty."

"Misconceptions," she murmured. Something flitted across her face.

He wondered at the change in her expression. It hit him that although their relationship had turned on its head because of Dorothy's stroke, making her a much bigger part of his life and his daily routine than she would have otherwise been, he still had a lot to learn about Tessa. She'd never spoken about her divorce, or her marriage for that matter. What had caused the divorce? And did she still love her ex-husband? All he actually knew was that she'd never had children. As much as she seemed to enjoy Poppy, he wondered why Tessa hadn't chosen to have children of her own. Or had the marriage always been rocky? Not wanting to share his own personal life, it was difficult for him to ask Tessa about hers.

But there were so many blanks. Ones that continued to remain empty. He hated that he itched to fill in those blanks. He summoned a picture of Lucy to mind, but instead of the endearing expression he was accustomed to imagining, he saw a question on her face, a hint of disapproval. Because he was thinking of another woman? Or because he hadn't learned more about the woman who was caring for Poppy?

And why was her face dimming just a fraction? It had always been so clear, so immediate.

"Which one's your favorite?" Poppy asked Tessa.

"Oh." She stared out into the fields, lifting and twisting around. "It's hard to choose, but I think the bluebonnets."

"When your parents visit, you should show them the wildflowers," Morgan suggested.

Tessa looked surprised.

Poppy grinned. "Will they be here tomorrow?"

"No." Tessa shook her head. "I haven't planned their visit."

"Why?" Poppy questioned.

Yes. Why? He wondered as well, finally drawn from his thoughts about Lucy's image.

"I've been pretty busy," Tessa explained.

Morgan thought of how he and Poppy monopolized Tessa's time. He hadn't considered the relationships she'd had to neglect because of that. "We shouldn't be consuming your days to the point that you can't visit with your parents." He frowned. "I thought you were going to have them visit some time ago."

She shrugged. "I haven't gotten around to fixing up the guest room in my cottage. They can visit later on."

He blinked, realizing how little free time she'd had to get truly settled in the cottage. "You don't have to wait for your guest room to be ready. There's plenty of space in the house for your parents to stay."

"They might feel awkward staying at your house," she objected.

"Not if you're there, too," he insisted. "We have several guest rooms. The whole point of the big house is to be able to entertain a lot of people."

"With Dorothy gone—"

"It won't be the same, but the place is reasonably kempt and Nancy will cook."

"Now can they come tomorrow?" Poppy asked eagerly.

Tessa finally smiled. "Not tomorrow, sweetheart, but I'll call them today and ask when they can visit."

Morgan wasn't sure why he'd pushed so hard for the visit, but Tessa's dedication seemed to merit it. Besides, he needed a happy occasion to look forward to. Briefly, he thought of the soured land deal. He would make some inquiries. And in the meantime, a thorough search of his study seemed like a good idea. He'd known that some corporate hounds were keen enough to use surveillance on their competitors. Not that he expected to uncover a bug, but it was only good sense to keep watch. He'd always felt the house was as secure as one could get. But that was before strangers had been hired for close positions. Nancy and Heather seemed like nice women, but he really didn't know enough about them to be absolutely sure they were worthy of his trust. He was glad that the treacherous nanny was gone. His only regret was not getting back her house key. And

Tessa... If she was working for another camp, she had earned herself an award for her performance.

The city park had become Poppy's favorite place to picnic. Now they were coming here a few times a week, and it wasn't getting old. Instead, Poppy got more excited each time. She loved the playground equipment; the slide was her first choice. But she loved the swings and monkey bars, as well.

Beneath the outstretched limbs of the ancient oak, Tessa and Poppy spread the plaid blanket, choosing to sit on the grass rather than at a table. Together they set the basket down. Tessa had tucked some juice boxes and sodas along with sandwiches and fruit into their wicker hamper. She remembered how her own mother had packed similar lunches when they'd gone on picnics, oftentimes frying chicken in a way that just she had. Feeling nostalgic, Tessa was glad that her parents would be visiting.

Both were community volunteers and had to set up their replacements for the trip. Smiling, Tessa could remember that it had been easier to take an impromptu journey when they were working full-time than it was now. Not that they had the wandering bug. They enjoyed being at home, feeling the permanence of where they had settled.

Cindy called out and waved from her car. With little Katy in tow, she joined them. "I still feel guilty that you brought everything," Cindy greeted her.

"Can we do the slide?" Poppy asked, bouncing lightly from foot to foot.

Checking Cindy's expression, Tessa gave them the go-ahead. "Not too long, though. We have lunch to eat."

Poppy and Katy bolted before she completely finished the last sentence.

"We can always reel them in later," Cindy said companionably as she sat on the blanket. "If I don't let Katy run off her initial excitement, she's a regular jumping bean during lunch. So, have you set a date for your parents' visit?"

"Close." Tessa explained their need to provide replacements for their volunteer jobs. "It's dicey because we don't know when Dorothy will come home."

"Any improvement?"

"The speech therapist at the rehab center is a wonder. It's still a struggle for Dorothy to talk, but she can speak so much more than she did in the hospital."

"Long-term prognosis?"

Tessa shrugged. "They still don't know. I keep praying for a full recovery, but I think Morgan's just happy that he's not going to lose her."

"Understandable," Cindy agreed, tossing her red hair back over one shoulder. "Dorothy and Alvin have been part of his life literally forever. You haven't mentioned whether Morgan's still giving you a hard time about taking Poppy to church."

Tessa thought of all the tension each and every weekend. By Saturday afternoon, the unspoken subject hung in the air. And by Sunday morning, Morgan was scowling. He hadn't forbidden the weekly outing, but he made his disapproval clear. "He still doesn't like it."

"I'd hoped by now that knowing you would have made it easier."

"Do we really know each other that well?" Tessa asked, retrieving two cans of root beer, handing one to Cindy.

"Funny thing to say."

"All I really know about Morgan is work and his child. Whatever else he's thinking he keeps inside."

Cindy popped the tab on her drink. "It's always hard for Flynn to talk about Julia. It's hard for *me* to talk about her, and she was my sister. I have true faith—I know I will see her again—but her loss still seems so…difficult. I hate that fear ate her up and then her fears came true. She died so young, just like Lucy. Flynn felt guilty because his whole heart wasn't with Julia. Morgan may feel guilty because Lucy died when Poppy was born. I know that doesn't make sense, but men don't always make sense, do they? Maybe he believes that Lucy would still be alive if they hadn't had a baby. At the same time, I'm sure he wouldn't trade Poppy for anything."

Tessa glanced toward the slide, watching as the girls giggled and ran around to the ladder. "It's so complicated. I can't help thinking that it would be so much easier for Morgan if he still had his faith."

"Of course it would," Cindy replied without hesitation. "Part of the healing is learning to let go, to trust again. Isn't trust the very hardest thing to regain?"

Tessa knew Cindy meant her own lack of trust. "Point taken. But it's myself I don't trust, not the Lord."

"But not trusting keeps love out of your life," Cindy replied gently. "And you are a woman who needs love."

Tessa shook her head. "That's what friends and family are for."

"Love that allows you to blossom, to share the bottomless well of compassion that's you. I can see how much you care for Poppy, for everyone in Morgan's home. Tessa, I wish you could see how good you are with Poppy, how much she adores you. I guess what I'm saying is that if you think trust is the only path to happiness for Morgan, you have to see that it's your only path, as well."

Tessa felt the clutch of pain that thinking about Karl caused. But as though shoving that aside, warmth filled her as she considered Morgan. Remembering him sitting tall in the saddle caused a tremor in her insides that threatened to melt her reserve. What was it about a man who wore jeans and boots as well as a *GQ*-approved suit? Who sat the horse as though he'd ridden it each and every day? Whose dark eyes somehow deepened beyond ebony?

"Thinking about him?" Cindy questioned quietly.

Tessa couldn't reply as her friend's words tumbled through her thoughts. Surely her trust issues and his couldn't be the same. Could they?

Chapter Sixteen

Sherry opened her briefcase, then took out a computer tablet, clicking it on. "So there was a problem on the report last month?"

"Just on the casing head gas," Tessa replied. The office seemed especially quiet with Poppy not in it. Morgan had taken her to visit Dorothy again.

Progress was the word of the day for Dorothy. It was as though she wanted a new accomplishment to show Poppy for each visit. She could string more than a couple of words together now. And she'd indicated through Alvin that she wanted to be home when Tessa's parents visited in a month or so.

That would be fine with Tessa. She was still nervous about their visit. She wasn't certain why, but ever since her mother had insisted that Tessa and Morgan were of the same mind-set, she had obsessed over the words. She didn't need her mother coming to Rosewood and pointing out that Morgan was in fact single, handsome and great marriage material. At least her mother would see him that way.

Their circumstances were very different, she rationalized. Lucy had died, something she certainly hadn't chosen, wouldn't have chosen. But Karl's choice was irrefutable. He had thrown Tessa away like a discarded tissue. No muss, no fuss. He hadn't once contacted her, checked on her, cared about her fate. Not that she wanted him back, Tessa realized.

When she thought of her old life, one thing stood out. Deluded. How had she not seen that he was shallow, untrue? She had always wanted the kind of love that unequivocally outweighed everything else in her life. One that made their union as perfect as possible—not in a materialistic way, but a faithful way. One where they cared more about each other's happiness than their own. She thought of Morgan, of how he adored his late wife, how he said her name almost reverently. She guessed that if he found that kind of love again, he would make that woman a wonderful husband.

Her stomach knotted at the thought of Morgan with a new wife, a new woman. Silly, she told herself. At some point he would meet someone, fall in love. That woman would mother Poppy and the other children they would have.

Tessa's throat closed. It was the way things would happen. Should happen. Then why did it hurt so much to imagine?

"I adjusted the figures," Sherry told her.

Jerked back to reality, Tessa glanced blindly at her own computer screen. She'd have to trust Sherry because a film of tears was obscuring her vision. "Um…good. That's fine."

Sherry looked puzzled.

"It will work, I mean," Tessa added in a rush.

"Do you have any correspondence we can help with?" Sherry asked.

"Not really." Morgan preferred to keep the correspondence close at hand. Not that much was committed to paper that he considered confidential. Still, he wasn't comfortable allowing it out of their purview. "We have that under control."

"Where's your little helper today?" Sherry asked, pointing to the empty corner where Poppy usually played.

"Visiting Dorothy."

"Oh. How's she coming along?"

"Good, really good, actually. She's improved more than we expected since she's been in rehab. I think the prospect of coming home has her fueled to do her therapy to the max."

"Isn't she kind of old to be coming back to a housekeeping job?"

Tessa straightened her spine, not liking the other woman's choice of words. "This is Dorothy's home."

"Of course. I just feel bad for her. That's a hard job even for a younger woman." Sherry shrugged. "I'd hate to see her be recovering and then have to tackle all the work of keeping up a big house."

Tessa couldn't pinpoint what she objected to, but

she didn't like Sherry's inference. "I don't think she sees it that way."

"Maybe Morgan will keep Heather on," Sherry mused. "That would help."

"I think that's the plan," Tessa acknowledged. Feeling much the way she had when discovering Janet at the Houston office, Tessa didn't want to say too much. "Main thing is we're glad she's getting better."

"Of course. I'm sure Poppy really misses her."

"We all do."

Sherry made a few more notes. "Okay, I think I have everything." She held up a sheaf of papers. "If anything else comes in, let me know."

"Sounds good." Tessa hesitated. "Thanks for doing all this extra work. You and Janet have been great."

Sherry smiled. "Just part of the job."

Tessa wondered if she had taken Sherry the wrong way that first encounter. If so, maybe that impression was coloring how she reacted ever since. The woman had been nothing but helpful. If she and Janet hadn't pitched in, everything would be hopelessly behind. "It's appreciated." The phone rang and she wasn't surprised to see that it was Janet, who asked if Sherry was still there. "She's just leaving." Tessa looked up at Sherry. "No, we're all set."

"Do I need to call Janet?" Sherry asked as Tessa hung up the phone.

"No. She just wanted to be sure we had everything taken care of."

"Janet's a great boss," Sherry murmured.

"That's good."

"She's so personally connected to the work," Sherry continued. "I guess she feels she's doing something for Morgan."

Tessa listened for any undertone but didn't hear one. Perhaps working closely with Janet, the other woman had a better picture of her than anyone else. "I suppose so."

Footsteps clattered in the entry hall.

"Sounds like the troops are here," Sherry joked. "I'll let myself out."

There was an undercurrent of voices and then the front door closed.

"Tessa!" Poppy called out, running toward the study.

"In here!" Tessa replied, smiling as the child sped inside.

"We're going riding!" Poppy announced. "And you can go, too!"

"Whoa. Did you have lunch?"

"Uh-huh. We got to eat at the café. And I got a cookie."

"How was Dorothy?"

"She can say more stuff now."

Tessa smiled. "I bet she liked the flowers you brought her."

"Daddy says she's going to come home soon."

"Really?" Tessa was surprised he'd told Poppy. He had confided that he thought with her progress Dorothy might be able to come home soon but had asked her not to mention it to Poppy, not wanting to get her hopes up too early. Something must have confirmed the notion, or he wouldn't have told Poppy.

"Chatterbox," Morgan said affectionately as he trailed into the office. "She's right, though. Dorothy's making such strides that her doctor believes she can come home soon, provided she gets therapy visits."

"Can that be arranged?" Tessa questioned hopefully.

"Already in process. She's conquered swallowing most things. Her voice is almost completely back. Weaker but back. And her movement's good. Luckily their rooms here are on the main floor, so she can get around in a wheelchair when she's too tired to walk."

"That's wonderful!" Tessa exclaimed.

Poppy clapped her hands. "Yay!"

"When she does come home, we can't overtax her," Morgan warned Poppy. "We can't ask her to do things she did before."

Puzzled, Poppy drew her eyebrows together. "Like what?"

Morgan looked momentarily at a loss so Tessa spoke. "Like baking. Nancy will still be here to cook."

"But Dorothy makes cookies with me."

"I know." Tessa took Poppy's hand. "And hopefully, she can do that again. Tell you what. If she can't, then I'll make cookies with you."

Poppy looked doubtful. "Do you know how?"

Tessa laughed. "I made cookies with my mother. I loved cutting out shapes."

"We have a heart one," Poppy remembered, referring to a cookie cutter.

Tessa lifted her gaze, meeting Morgan's. Realizing he was watching her, she warmed at the thought. What a notion, she told herself. He had to look somewhere. She had been speaking. But that didn't explain the deepening, mesmerizing expression.

"When is your mommy coming?" Poppy asked.

"What?" Tessa nervously straightened a small stack of papers. "Oh, they said they could come next month. If that's okay with everyone."

"It's okay with me," Poppy declared.

Tessa continued to hold Morgan's gaze and though he didn't speak, she didn't see a denial in sight.

Dorothy's return took three more weeks but it was finally the big day. Morgan thought Poppy might burst when they brought her home. He had contracted a carpenter to build ramps at both entrances. He wanted Dorothy to be able to get around as much as possible, certainly not to be trapped inside. Fortunately, the old house had many double doorways, so she could use a wheelchair when it was needed. She insisted on a cane for the ride home. But Morgan had spoken with her physical therapist. Although

Dorothy had walked in the rehab facility, that didn't prepare her for the long distances inside.

On discharge day, paperwork and instructions for home care seemed to take forever. Finally, Dorothy was free. And Poppy had bounced in her seat all the way home. Morgan watched as the house came into view. Peace that had been absent settled in Dorothy's features.

He had texted Tessa to let her know they were on the way. Poppy sat in back with Alvin, contained only by her booster seat belt. When they pulled up front, Tessa was standing at the bottom of the steps with the wheelchair he'd bought the day before.

"Morgan, you bought that?" Dorothy chided, her words taking longer to get out, but making their way.

"I'm going to donate the wheelchair when you don't need it any longer," he reassured her. "But we don't want to tire you out and set back your progress before you're fully recovered. I've no doubt you'll be running all over the house before long."

Dorothy's eyes were bright as she got out of the car then moved slowly toward the door.

"Welcome home!" Tessa said, her smile sunny.

Poppy carefully walked next to Dorothy, tamping down her usual zippy run.

"Alvin, I'll bring everything inside," Morgan told the older man, seeing the worry in his eyes as Dorothy neared the wheelchair. "Dorothy, how about we use the wheelchair to get in the house, then back to your rooms?"

She looked torn. "I guess so."

Relieved, Morgan guided her into the chair. Tessa tactfully reached for the cane and he pushed the wheelchair up the ramp.

Dorothy looked tentative until they were inside. Then her smile really blossomed. "Home."

Morgan patted her shoulder. "Not a second too soon."

"We've missed you," Tessa added. "You look great!"

"I don't know…about *great*." Dorothy spoke slowly.

"You look pretty," Poppy chimed in.

Dorothy reached out and Poppy slid into her hug. "I've missed you."

"I missed you more," Poppy declared.

Dorothy hugged her again.

Feeling overcome by all the feminine emotion, Morgan decided to clear the room. "Tessa, would you make sure the doors are open? Poppy, take the cane and carry it, please."

Pleased to have the responsibility, Poppy took the cane and pranced down the hall. Morgan knew the doors were open, but he needed to get the sticky emotional wave under control. If they all went to pieces, they wouldn't be doing Dorothy any favors. The nurse had told him that just returning to the house would be exhausting for Dorothy. That she would want to slip back into old routines and would think she was capable of doing more than she could. They were to watch her carefully so she didn't relapse.

Once installed in her own bedroom, Dorothy agreed to sit in one of the recliners.

"Our room never seemed so far back in the house," Dorothy admitted as she rose from the wheelchair.

"Just seems that way now," Morgan murmured. "Once you're settled in, things will feel more normal."

"I can't help wondering how I'll get back to being myself."

Morgan refrained from pointing out the obvious. If she fully considered how limited she was in regard to literally everything, she'd be overwhelmed. He reached for an afghan, laying it over her knees. "Your value's a lot more than what you cook and clean. I told you about both Nancy and Heather. They're here to make your job easier." Morgan lightly squeezed her shoulder in encouragement. "And we all can pitch in, as well. In fact, Tessa got your suite ready." He'd been touched that she wanted to. Tessa had insisted, filling vases with fresh flowers in each of their rooms, locating a pitcher and glasses for fresh lemon water.

"Looks really nice," Dorothy replied, glancing at Tessa. "Thank you."

"My pleasure. You've made me feel so welcome…" Tessa swallowed, still looking emotional. "Anyway, it's wonderful to have you home. Nancy will have lunch ready in about an hour. Morgan said you enjoy chicken potpie, so one's baking."

"I thought…I smelled…something good." Her voice was weakening more.

"Not as good as yours, but in a pinch it'll fill us up," Morgan insisted. He wanted Dorothy to rest, but knew she needed to feel relevant, necessary. "Alvin, why don't you settle yourself while I get the bags."

"I can—"

"Nope, I already called it." Morgan grinned. It was a phrase from the past, from his childhood.

Alvin looked as tired as Dorothy. "Just this one time."

How had he not noticed how much they had aged? Neither of them had ever complained about their workload, which he now realized had been far too large. Poppy leaned against Dorothy, who stroked her hair. Their love for his daughter was nearly as great as his own.

Glancing up, he met Tessa's gaze, seeing the contentment there. It was as though, without him knowing when or how, she had become part of their family. She belonged. She was trusted, cared for… more than cared for. Certainly more than he had ever bargained for.

Chapter Seventeen

With Dorothy settling back in, the house was in a pleasant whir, therapists, guests and a nurse visiting daily. Janet and Sherry continued coming in to assist since Tessa was still caring for Poppy. And their small staff, cook and cleaner and yardman, was still with them, hired on permanently.

Tessa enjoyed seeing Poppy's interaction with Dorothy. She was truly a grandmother figure in every way. Lucy's parents had been older when Lucy was born and had passed away before Poppy was in the picture. Poppy had her paternal grandparents, but Dorothy and Alvin had stepped in as the other set.

Although Dorothy tired easily, she seemed to love the time Poppy sat with her, holding books and telling tales from them since she couldn't yet read. She had colored several pages of drawings for Dorothy. They were stuck on the door of the small refrigerator Morgan had installed in the suite.

Tessa had watched him through the process of resettling Dorothy and Alvin, taking in his broad protective streak, the certainty he showed in all his actions.

Morgan had asked Tessa to find someone to assist Alvin. It wasn't easy, but she had employed all of Cindy's contacts. Frank's lawn service would continue, but Lance, the new general maintenance man, could help Alvin with all the other things the older man wanted to make sure were done. In the long run, Morgan had told her he believed Alvin would be happiest with the responsibility of keeping up the house, but not all the physical labor that came with the job. This way he could keep a close eye on Dorothy, yet keep himself busy and motivated, and be certain the house was secure.

And that seemed especially important to Morgan. Tessa wondered why. Harper Petroleum didn't employ high security and, as far as she knew, it'd never had any threats to its operations. Maybe it was all just because of Poppy, Tessa reasoned. No doubt after losing Lucy, he was afraid he could somehow lose Poppy, too. Thinking of the fierce protectiveness he had demonstrated, Tessa didn't envy anyone who threatened her safety.

But in Rosewood, safety seemed a certain thing. People still left their doors unlocked, many businesses had trust policies. At the dairy and egg, there was a collection box where people deposited the money for the goods they picked up. And she thought of the tack room at the stable, where some very expensive saddles were stored without worry of theft.

After Dorothy's return, the community embraced them in a comforting way. Every single day at least one person dropped by with a casserole, dessert or freshly baked bread, a treat of some form. Other visitors came often enough to make certain they spelled Alvin, yet stayed out of the way of therapists. Anything they needed was at hand just for the asking.

Cindy had continued to invite Poppy to the Rainbow class. She also had them over for playdates. Preschool was too far along, too close to being done for the year, so that wasn't a viable option at this point. The teacher had suggested that they teach Poppy some basics, then enroll her in September for the coming year. The preschool offered a class for five-year-olds who hadn't had any previous schooling, and by then Poppy would fit that description.

"I thought kids learned that stuff in kindergarten," Morgan mused as he flipped through the morning mail.

"We used to," Tessa admitted. "But without preschool, kids have a disadvantage. The others already know their letters, numbers, some essentials. I could read and print when I went to kindergarten."

"A whiz kid?" he questioned, his mouth edging up in a smile.

"No. An only child with parents who liked spending a lot of time with me."

"Speaking of which, when do your parents visit?"

"Next weekend." She frowned. "Unless that's not convenient."

"I'm getting the impression that you don't want them to meet us."

Shocked, she hoped he was teasing. "That's not it."

"Then what is it?"

Not able to tell him, she switched tracks. "Cindy invited Poppy to the Rainbow class again."

Morgan's expression slid from amused to puzzled. "Do I want to know what it's about?"

"It's a class Cindy organized for kids who need a little extra attention. Not that she thinks Poppy has any issues. It's just so she can be around the kids, take part in the class activities."

"And where does this class meet?"

Rats, she was hoping he wouldn't ask. "You know the building where they hold receptions at the church?"

He frowned. "Is there nothing to do in Rosewood that isn't connected to church?"

"I have one good friend in this town. You know Cindy attends church and so do her friends. We need her help getting Poppy the interaction we want. Surely you still don't think participation at church is a bad thing?"

"Can you give me one reason that should have changed my mind?"

"You have a host of blessings," she rallied. "Can't you see that? A beautiful daughter, loving parents, Dorothy and Alvin, all the people who work for you."

"A fair exchange for Lucy?"

"I didn't say that." At once bristling and chastened, she felt her breath coming in deep gulps. Morgan would never get over the love he felt for Lucy. No woman would ever reside in his heart again. Certainly not one like her, one who couldn't give him more children. Trying to settle her breathing, she clutched the edge of the desk. "Does that mean Poppy can't attend?"

He exhaled. "No. She can go. Ronnie Broussard should be here soon."

Feeling she had little to lose, Tessa voiced what she'd been thinking for some time. "He would make an excellent manager, someone you could hand over part of the management responsibilities to. And you could cultivate his assistant to take over his field duties."

"Have you already had a revised corporate ladder chart drawn up?" he questioned.

"I know you think you have to do everything." She paused, knowing she was taking the biggest risk yet. "But being there for every single decision won't ensure your employees' jobs. If you burn out, Harper could be compromised." Again she hesitated. "Morgan, it's not your fault. Lucy, I mean. You couldn't have saved her."

A muscle twitched in his jaw. "Tread very softly."

"Dorothy told me what happened. If the doctors couldn't prevent what happened, how could you?"

"Because I knew something was wrong. The doctors said I was imagining things. I should have insisted."

"Insisting wouldn't have mattered," she replied gently. "It was spontaneous, sudden. All the tests in the world couldn't have stopped it."

"Easy for you to say."

She took another deep breath. "Hardly."

"Seems a lot in your life is easy. Look how easily you walked away from your marriage."

"Easily?" she breathed, rising from her chair, hardly able to speak. "Easily?"

He swiped one hand across his brow. "You're right. I don't know how you feel about your divorce. You haven't said another word about it since the day of your interview."

"Do you suppose that might be because I don't want to? That it's, in fact, not easy?"

"Yet my talking about Lucy is?"

She sank back in her chair. "Nothing about either is easy. But ignoring my divorce isn't hurting a child."

"I'm hurting Poppy?"

"Your lack of faith," she replied, her voice gentling. "Haven't you considered that she needs faith in her life, too? That keeping it from her isn't right?"

"You know an awful lot about children, considering you don't have any of your own."

Though he didn't know it, the blow hit right on target. Deflated, she didn't have the strength to fight this out with him anymore. "Is it still all right for me to take Poppy to the Rainbow class?"

He waved his hand in frustration. "Fine."

Pain ricocheted, his words running over and again through her mind. He was right, of course. She would never have a child to guide, to teach. She wished suddenly that she hadn't asked her parents to visit. One thing had become clear. Despite her ridiculous feelings for Morgan, for Poppy, for the happiness she'd found in Rosewood, she wasn't in the right place. Not unless she wanted her heart to splinter beyond repair.

Morgan finished up his meeting with Ronnie Broussard, pleased that the other man had so many good ideas, even better solutions. Tessa's suggestion taunted him. Could he really give Ronnie an executive position? His father and grandfather had always been the sole executives in Harper's chain of command. But then each had a wife who cared for his children. Morgan had always thought he did a pretty good job of single parenting. Of course, it would have been better for Poppy to have both a mother and a father. Irrationally he thought of Tessa, how good she was with Poppy, how naturally the role fit her. But she hadn't said a solitary word about why she didn't have children.

From the way she'd shut down when he mentioned her divorce, it was apparently still a sensitive issue. She'd been clear that first day in telling him that

Houston wasn't big enough to hold her and her ex. Was she still in love with him? His gut knotted. It was an ugly thought.

"Daddy?"

Pulled from his thoughts, he looked down at his daughter. "What are you up to, termite?"

She climbed into his lap. "Can we go get ice cream?"

He winced. "It's not all that long until dinner. It'll spoil your appetite."

Poppy shook her tiny head. "Nuh-uh. We get it sometimes after we go to riding."

He wasn't up to a ride today, to seeing Beauty, knowing what she represented, then feeling Lucy's image fade just a bit more. He couldn't pinpoint when that had begun, but her face dimmed, then dimmed again. Silly, when he could walk to the credenza and see a framed picture of his late wife. But he never used to have to do that. Her face had always surfaced in his thoughts as though he'd seen her just that day. So many days had passed. More than four years of them. For so long, each had blurred into the next, but not Lucy. Her image had remained sharp, fixed in his mind.

"So can we?"

Blankly he stared at her.

"I want a chocolate one."

Ice cream. He remembered now. Suddenly, it seemed as good a diversion as any other. He didn't want to think about why Lucy's image was fading, why his thoughts were filled with Tessa. In a blink he could envision her remarkable eyes, the sway of her hair over her shoulders when she left it loose, how totally female she was in her gauzy cotton dresses. No, thinking of ice cream was much safer, certainly saner.

After dinner Tessa visited with Dorothy and Alvin. Dorothy had walked to the dining room, but looked pretty tired, so Tessa fetched the wheelchair.

"Your parents...visit?" Dorothy asked.

"I was hoping you'd go over the menu with me," Tessa replied, wanting to include Dorothy in the plans. "I know what they like but I thought you could suggest some regional dishes."

"German...Polish."

"And Czech," Tessa added, seeing how hard the words were coming for Dorothy. "I thought we could work on it tomorrow morning before therapy if that works for you."

Dorothy nodded, looking exhausted.

Tessa bit her lip, wondering if the task was too much. She glanced over at Alvin, who gave her a discreet thumbs-up. Relieved, Tessa pushed Dorothy the rest of the way into their sitting room. "I think I'll say good-night. It's been a long day." As she started to leave the room, she heard the doorbell ring. "Looks like it's not over."

Morgan had taken Poppy to dinner at the café, but he wouldn't ring the doorbell.

Opening the door, Tessa was surprised to see Janet standing in the doorway. "Hello." She opened the door wider. "Come in."

"Sorry to bother you. I think I left my card case here, the little black aluminum case I carry my debit and credit card in. I spilled my purse and thought I got everything, but when I stopped at the grocery store I realized the case wasn't in my purse. Do you mind if I look for it?"

"Of course not. I'll help."

"I hate to bother you in the evening."

"You're not," Tessa replied truthfully. "I truly don't have a single plan."

"Your little shadow?" Janet questioned.

"Poppy's with Morgan. They ate out." Tessa led the way into the office. "Let's see. You were sitting on this side of Morgan's desk, right?"

"Yes. I was on this side and Sherry was across from me, using Morgan's computer since she forgot her tablet."

"Right." Tessa hadn't worried since Morgan's files were password encoded. Sherry couldn't have looked at them if she wanted to.

Janet pushed in the wooden shelf, then looked on the floor. "Funny. I don't see it."

Tessa joined her, helping move the other chair out of the way, but nothing sat upon the lush silk rug other than furniture. "Could you have lost it somewhere else?"

Janet drew her eyebrows together. "I can't imagine

where. I don't use the case all the time, just when I need my debit or credit card. Do you mind if I look in your office? I went in there to get the call log."

"Go right ahead."

The phone rang. Deciding to be discreet, Tessa crossed the room and answered the call out in the entry hall. Since it was Cindy, she talked for a few moments, then promised to call her friend back.

Reentering the study, she saw Janet emerge from the adjacent office. "No luck."

"Can you remember when you had it last?"

Janet glanced down, thinking. "I had it two days ago when I went to lunch. I brought a salad from home today, so I didn't need it earlier. Well, I'll look in my car and at the office. Sorry to bother you."

"No bother. Hope you find it."

"I'm sure I will. Just felt silly at the store, filling my basket, then not being able to pay."

"I hope the rest of your evening is better."

A bleak look darted onto Janet's face before she smoothed her expression. "It'll be like all my evenings." She issued a humorless laugh. "Good night, then."

Pushing the door closed, Tessa leaned against it for a moment, remembering all she had heard about Janet. She looked so unhappy. Was she really still in love with Morgan? Could she have carried a torch all these years? Thinking of her own feelings, Tessa swallowed.

Chapter Eighteen

Morgan had begun thinking that Tessa didn't want her parents to visit. The date had been changed twice since it was supposedly set.

Now that the day was here for their visit, he was more curious than he should be. City slickers, he thought with a small smile, realizing belatedly that he was acting as though that was what he expected. Knowing he was making too much of the postponements for their visit, he came out of his study when he heard voices in the entry hall.

Poppy was already launched into the midst of their visitors. Remembering his first impression of Tessa, he expected sleek sophistication. Instead, her father was dressed in jeans and her mother wore a casual cotton top and skirt. But it was their smiles that captured his attention. Both had friendliness filling their expressions, exuding from every gesture.

"Edward Pierce," the gentleman told him, extending a hand.

Morgan shook his hand, seeing that the amicability extended to his eyes. "Then you must be…"

"Sheila," a more mature version of Tessa chimed in, taking his hand. "So good to meet you." She smiled down at Poppy. "And you are just as pretty as Tessa told me."

Grinning, Poppy looked from Sheila to Tessa.

"I'll introduce you to Dorothy and Alvin in a bit," Tessa added.

Morgan guessed that Tessa had filled them in on Dorothy's situation. "I hope our little town doesn't bore you."

"Have you been to Magnolia?" Edward asked. "Until Houston spread to the outskirts, it was barely a bump in the road. Now it's just a slightly bigger bump, the way we like it."

"Tessa told me you'd left the city."

"Living in Houston was great when we were younger," Sheila mused. "But we always dreamed of living in the country. Problem is the country keeps getting gobbled up."

"One reason we keep things simple here." He rested his hands on Poppy's shoulders to slow her emphatic bouncing. "Although I understand that Tessa has a full roster of activities set up for you."

"We're going to ride horses," Poppy exclaimed. Turning, she grabbed Morgan's hand. "Aren't we, Daddy?"

He gazed at Tessa in question. "Are we?"

"You mentioned taking them to see the wildflowers," Tessa reminded him.

So he had. He glanced at his watch.

Poppy tugged his hand, pulling the watch out of view. "Come on, Daddy."

"Now?"

"I thought I'd show them to their rooms first," Tessa replied, tilting her head slightly, the look in her eyes clear.

"Of course." Well, there was no getting out of the ride. Her look had been pure female, one that had men complying for aeons.

While their guests freshened up, Morgan made a few calls. He was surprised when Janet wasn't in the office to give him her usual update. But Sherry was helpful.

The SUV was full as they drove to the stables. Poppy had a great time entertaining Edward and Sheila during the ride. It occurred to him that his daughter had somehow inherited Lucy's outgoing personality.

Glancing over at Tessa, he caught her watching him. "What?"

She shook her head.

"What?" he repeated.

"You didn't have to come along." She fiddled with her seat belt, then thumped her hands to an uneasy rest.

Fortunately the conversation in the back row kept their voices covered. "I know."

Tessa looked at him again, her eyes questioning.

He understood the unspoken query. No, they weren't in a romantic relationship, so he could have gotten out of the ride. But the line between professional and personal had blurred so early on that it no longer existed. They'd never talked about the changes, the fact that their lives were so intertwined. He sneaked another glance at her profile. Long lashes dipped as she bent her head, her lips were pursed. Clearly she enjoyed a good relationship with her parents, yet thought they would interpret his absence as significant.

"We can ride beyond the fields once we see the flowers," he offered.

Tessa brightened. "Oh?"

"To the view of the live oak grove. No narrow trails, just a gentle incline on a wide plain." He didn't have to add that the setting wouldn't induce her fear of heights.

Only a few minutes later, they were at the stable. As they piled out of the car, he considered how many horses he owned. Five, with five people to ride.

Comfortable with tack, Edward and Sheila were soon saddling the horses he chose for each. That left Duke, Cornflake and Beauty. Once Cornflake was securely saddled, he swallowed past the lump in his throat that Beauty always caused.

"I'll rent a horse," Tessa decided, turning toward the small office next to the barn.

"That's not necessary." He patted Beauty. "We have enough horses."

"But that's…." She didn't go on.

"I know. Something tells me Lucy wouldn't mind." It was a wrench saddling the mare. He remembered how happy Lucy had been when he'd bought Beauty, how the two always seemed a perfect fit. He wondered what Lucy would think of Tessa, not just riding her horse, but caring for her daughter.

Once all the horses were saddled, he watched as Tessa mounted Beauty. The mare nickered as Tessa got her seat. Beauty didn't protest, turning her head to look at Morgan.

Doing his best to push the past aside, he took his own place on Duke, then led their intrepid party through the fields. With summer close at hand, wild grass fluttered tall and frothy in the meadows. The flowers bloomed year-round, changing with the seasons, but always peppering the landscape. However, today his attention was drawn to Tessa.

She was a different person around her parents. Completely relaxed, her smile easy and frequent, she seemed at peace. Why was that? he wondered. Why did she tense up otherwise?

Well, not always, he acknowledged. She was easygoing around Poppy. Most especially when she didn't know he was watching.

Was he the fly in the ointment? The one person who made her stiffen, become wary?

Subtly slowing Duke, Morgan studied Tessa atop

Beauty. They went together perfectly, which startled him. He'd always thought his blonde, blue-eyed wife was the perfect foil for Beauty. How was it someone so different could also look so right?

Poppy's laugh tinkled into the breeze, her gaiety much like the wildflowers, brightening everything around her. Tessa was especially bright today, Morgan realized. Unrestrained, natural, she was as appealing as the hills that beckoned beyond, as beautiful as the bursts of wildflowers. Bluebonnets bloomed near her and Morgan didn't have to be within reach to know how her eyes would react, how they would be enhanced.

He felt a curtain fall away. His interest wasn't platonic, not that of just a boss. When had that last slip occurred? When had he started seeing Tessa as…a woman?

The distinct, often admired landscape of the Hill Country didn't disappoint as they rode for the next two hours. But Morgan didn't notice, his attention completely captivated by Tessa.

Tessa slipped a few pages into a correspondence folder. So little had to be committed to paper these days, but she had always kept a reader file, one that contained all the correspondence Morgan generated and all his interoffice memorandums as well as copies of his incoming correspondence. The backup file was a holdover from older traditions, but it had saved her on more than one occasion when an original letter was misfiled.

"Tessa!" Poppy called out as she skidded into the room.

"You're supposed to be in bed," she responded, unable to summon a chiding note to her voice. Instead she held out her arms. "I read one extra book and sang two extra songs." She smoothed the hair from Poppy's forehead, tucked another lock behind one ear. "What's keeping you awake?"

"I kept waiting for you to come to bed."

"Oh." While her parents were visiting, Tessa was staying in the nanny room next to Poppy instead of in the cottage. "You know I come down to work for a while after you go to sleep."

"I don't want you to work," Poppy said, nestling against her.

"You don't?"

"Nuh-uh. Just be my mommy."

Tessa's breath caught and she tightened her arms around Poppy. Knowing that would never happen, she wondered at the harm she was doing letting that fantasy take shape. "Sweetheart, you know I love you, but I can't be your mommy."

"How come?" Poppy asked, her voice sleepy.

"Well...one day your daddy may find a lady, a nice lady, to love. Then she would become your mommy." Tessa struggled with the words, knowing they were true, provided Morgan moved past the loss of his wife.

"I only want you," Poppy insisted.

And Tessa wanted only Poppy and Morgan. It was true. Despite her disastrous marriage, her faulty sense of trust, she had allowed her heart to run wild. Irony hit. Cindy had run away to Rosewood and naively Tessa had done the same. Tessa wondered about her own motives. Had she subconsciously hoped that she would have a fairy-tale ending much like Cindy's? She thought of the pain her friend had endured, the loss of her sister that would always hurt. No, not fairy-tale, but still happy.

The difference was faith, Tessa realized. Flynn had come back to his, and that alone had lifted his blinders, letting him find love with Cindy. But that couldn't happen with Morgan.

Taking Poppy's hand in hers, Tessa led her back upstairs. Tucking her in, singing a lullaby until eyelids closed, Tessa couldn't stop thinking. How could she continue here? She could cherish Poppy's love for a lifetime, but to wait on the sidelines, much like Janet Divo, as Morgan found someone to love? Just the thought was shattering. The reality would be even worse.

Yet how could she leave? She cared about every occupant of the house. Dorothy and Alvin were just getting settled back in. And Dorothy was in no condition to care for Poppy. Abandoning the child wasn't even thinkable.

She smoothed the blanket, tucking it over one outstretched arm. Poppy didn't even stir. So trusting, so loving. Tessa swallowed, never wanting any harm or hurt to come to this child.

The people she cared most about in the world were all under this roof tonight. How was she going to resolve this? She imagined her parents along with Dorothy and Alvin as she'd left them in the family room all visiting. Her mother, always a natural in any social situation, had engaged Dorothy immediately, latching on to one of their favorite topics, crafts.

Reluctantly Tessa left Poppy's room, then descended the stairs. Seeing that her mother and Dorothy were still chatting, she wondered where Morgan and her father had gotten to.

"Nice place you've got here," Edward told Morgan as they strolled the perimeter of the property.

"Can't take credit for it," Morgan admitted. "The family started with one cottage, then built the house once the business was established. The other cottages were built in intervals after that. The setup has worked for a lot of years."

"There's much to be said for continuity," Edward agreed. "When we retired, Sheila and I thought our place would be for a lifetime."

Morgan sensed something was left unsaid. "But it's not?"

"We bought the land twenty years ago when Magnolia wasn't in anyone's sights. Back then it was pure country. Of course that was a lot of years before we built the house. That didn't happen until we retired. By then we had the land paid for and we thought we'd picked a spot too far away for the city to grow into us."

"But it has."

Edward nodded. "Now with Tessa living here, we can't help wondering what's holding us."

Morgan remained quiet, sensing there was a question yet unasked.

"Does Tessa seem happy here to you?" Edward asked finally.

"Happy?" *Was she?*

"Karl did a number on her," Edward replied. "Can't say I blame her for leaving the city, especially since they both worked for United."

Morgan blinked, then drew his eyebrows together. "Tessa told me she worked for Traxton."

"Which United bought. They kept the original name since United is out of New York and Traxton's a good brand here in Texas. But they answer to United."

His nemesis. "Why have they kept the sale under wraps?"

Edward tipped his head, considering. "It was a private sale and they kept on all the executive staff. There's probably a footnote somewhere in the *Journal* about the purchase. I wouldn't have known if Tessa didn't work for Traxton."

"And her ex-husband works there, as well?" Morgan felt as though he'd been sucker punched. It was his own fault that he hadn't kept up on the buyout. If he had more executive level staff he'd have been informed.

"That's how they met." Edward paused. "Karl transferred to another division, acquisitions."

Acquisitions? Morgan immediately thought of the coveted leases that Traxton had just outmaneuvered him on. "Is he valuable to United?"

Edward shrugged. "If it benefits him. Karl's not the kind of person to be concerned about who he steps on if they're in the way. Never understood why Tessa settled for him."

His mind switched gears. "Settled?"

"You know Tessa by now. I don't think it's just parental pride to say she's pretty special."

Morgan remained silent. Inwardly he agreed.

"And Karl…isn't," Edward continued. "Oh, he's good-looking, has plenty of charm. But Tessa deserves more."

"He doesn't sound that bad," Morgan said cautiously, wondering if the ex-husband would use Tessa to get a business advantage.

"Bad? No." Edward stared into the darkness. "But not good enough. Can't verbalize it, but there it is."

"I guess Tessa agrees since they divorced."

Edward tipped his head, studying Morgan. "She doesn't talk about it that much?"

"At all," Morgan admitted.

"Then I won't, either." Edward turned back toward

the house. "I suppose my wife and daughter will be wondering where I am."

"Tessa's put Poppy to bed," Morgan acknowledged as they walked.

"She's sure taken by your little one." Edward shook his head.

"What?"

"Nothing. Just good to see that side of Tessa. She's always been tenderhearted. Nice to see how it comes out with Poppy."

"I thought Tessa was all about her career when she first came here," Morgan admitted.

Edward smiled. "She does sophisticated really well. That's Sheila's influence. She was a model back in the day."

Morgan thought of Mrs. Pierce, how attractive she still was. "It's not hard to see why."

Edward's smile widened. "My girls have kept me on my toes. When Tessa first began dating, I practically rode shotgun. I wouldn't have let Karl past my radar on my watch. But she met him after college."

Morgan smiled, but questions were bubbling. He hated what he was thinking, suspecting.

Chapter Nineteen

Tessa couldn't shake the image of Morgan's expression as they'd all left to attend church. Betrayal. She'd seen it in his eyes. Stomach lurching, she wondered if insisting on Poppy's attendance was driving him further away.

Sitting through Sunday school, then church service, the minutes dragged. Her parents, enchanted with Rosewood, were equally taken by the Victorian church and friendly congregation.

However, Tessa kept examining her motives for trying to reconnect Morgan to his faith. She knew each person's path was unique, that the tenets of faith were inherently individual. Even as she reexamined what she'd done and said, Tessa knew she hadn't pushed Morgan for selfish or personally motivated reasons. She was certain he would be happier when back in touch with his faith. Just knowing that he would eventually be reunited with his one true love should be a comfort. Pain ruptured in her heart. She wondered what kind of woman he would eventually choose, provided he got over Lucy. Heart tight, she knew it certainly wouldn't be her.

Dorothy had agreed to the wheelchair. The conveyance made attendance possible since the church building was large, spread out. She couldn't have walked all the necessary corridors. As it was, she was exhausted by the time they returned home.

"Dorothy, would you like a tray?" Tessa asked her quietly, privately.

The older woman finally nodded.

"You'll build up your strength," Tessa assured her. "I know you will."

Dorothy grasped Tessa's hand and squeezed it weakly in appreciation.

Knowing all the older woman had gone through, Tessa was touched by her gratitude. Dorothy was terribly self-sufficient and it hadn't been easy to accept help.

Nancy had been coaxed to come in to cook even though it was Sunday since Tessa's parents were visiting. She had arrived early to bake a ham and prepare side dishes that could be reheated. Tessa saw that she'd also set the table for lunch in the dining room.

With Dorothy and Alvin eating in their rooms, that left only five for lunch. Tessa picked up the two extra place settings, then lingered over a third, wondering if Morgan would join them.

It was only fair to tell him that Dorothy and Alvin were eating alone.

Tessa found him where she expected, in the office.

He nodded. "Playing catch-up. Just got off the phone with Ronnie."

She grasped the top rung of the chair she usually sat in. "Have you given any more thought to promoting him? Getting some help with your workload?"

"Any special reason you're zeroing in on Ronnie?"

She blinked. "Just the confidence you have in him." The East Texas area had the largest output, was their biggest moneymaker. "Why?"

Morgan looked down at the document on his desk. "Did you need something?"

"Yes." She remembered the reason for her mission. "Are you joining us for lunch?" Tessa hesitated. "Dorothy and Alvin are eating in their rooms."

"So you wanted to warn me off?"

She frowned. "No. Just thought it was fair to tell you. I'm sure my parents would enjoy having lunch with you and Poppy."

"Fine, then."

Tessa gripped the chair harder, then let her hand fall away. "Yes, fine. I'm reheating the lunch Nancy made. Should be ready soon." She started to turn away.

"I won't be here for dinner."

"Oh?"

"I have a survey to take to the Houston office."

"Right." She nodded. "You can't use a messenger, I suppose?"

"Would have to be somebody I really *trust*," he responded, emphasizing the last word.

She considered, then exhaled. "I could go if you really need me to."

"While your parents are here visiting?"

"Truthfully? I'd rather not, but I'll go if it's needed."

Morgan stared at her. "No. I'll go."

She wondered at the heaviness in his voice.

Lunch was an uneven affair. Her parents kept the conversation alive. Although Tessa tried her best to contribute, she was distracted. Morgan was unusually quiet, and her attention wandered toward him.

"I'm glad you stayed over," Tessa said, catching her father's gaze. "There's always so much traffic on Sunday nights, people going back into the city." She glanced at Morgan. He would be part of that mob.

"We want one more stroll down Main Street tomorrow before we go back," Sheila chimed in. "I saw a wood carving I think I can't live without."

Tessa met Morgan's gaze, surprised to see how intense it was.

Edward groaned. "I had a feeling we'd be bringing something back."

"Be glad it's not the armoire," Sheila retorted. "We saw a beautiful one. Really unusual piece, by Matt Whitaker. Someone said he's a well-known designer. But I couldn't think of a place where I could put the piece."

Tessa dragged her gaze away from Morgan. "Sounds like a good idea."

Sheila looked from Tessa to Morgan. Then she widened her eyes at Edward. Noticing, Tessa wondered what she'd said wrong. "So, you're going to buy an armoire?"

"Not this time," Sheila replied.

Poppy giggled.

"What's funny?" Tessa questioned.

Poppy giggled again.

"You missed it," Edward improvised.

"Why don't we have some coffee," Tessa suggested, ready for the meal to end. She wished she knew what was bothering Morgan.

Morgan checked his watch. "I have some things to work on."

She hoped nothing was wrong. Was it because she'd mentioned promoting Ronnie Broussard? No, Morgan had been down before she had mentioned him. He had been brooding that morning. Then it had to be about church, she decided. He was upset that she was still taking Poppy to church.

It wasn't like him to hold on to his resentment. They'd bickered over the topic since her first days. But he'd never carried it with him.

Tessa realized she was distracted as she had coffee and kolaches with her parents. Poppy liked serving the small pastries, especially sorting out the cherry ones for herself.

"Do you mind if we take a walk?" her father asked.

"Of course not, Dad. I've got some work to check."

"Can I go?" Poppy asked.

Tessa glanced at her parents.

"Fine with us. We need a seasoned guide," Edward assured the hopeful tot.

"I can be it," Poppy attested, not knowing what a guide was.

Smiling, Tessa agreed.

"So you can still smile," her father said quietly.

"I'm kind of on edge," Tessa explained, hating to disappoint her parents. "Didn't mean for it to spoil your visit."

"Did I say that?" he chided.

She made her smile wider. "No. But you wouldn't."

"Whatever it is, Tessa, you'll find your answer."

"You're so sure there's a question?"

Edward patted her hand. "We won't be long."

"I'll help you load the dishwasher," Sheila offered.

"No! Go, enjoy your walk."

With plenty to check on, Tessa finished carrying in the lunch dishes. Her parents had each grabbed a stack, divvying up the work, so there was little left. It didn't take long to load the dishwasher. Not sure whether she wanted to disturb Morgan, she entered her office in a way she seldom ever did, through the side door in the entry hall.

Once she logged on to her computer, Tessa lost herself catching up with work that she'd had to postpone. Seeing a report that needed to be completed, she made a mental note to call Janet. Afraid she might forget, she wrote a quick email, marking it as important.

An hour later, encased in her solitary world of

work, she was startled to hear drawers slamming in Morgan's office. They continued. Alarmed, she crossed the space between their desks. "Is something wrong?"

He clenched his jaw. "You could say that."

She waited.

He glanced up, still not explaining.

"What?" She drew her head back. "What is it?"

"The survey in the bottom drawer."

Again she waited.

"It's gone."

"Gone?" she echoed. "You must have put it in a different place."

"No. It was in the bottom drawer."

"Maybe it got shoved out the back. Did you look under the desk?"

"It's gone," he stated again, his voice harder than she'd ever heard it.

"But that doesn't make sense." Tessa paused. "The surveys are confidential." Her words stumbled. "Which means no one knew about this one except you and me. If I thought you…"

"Tessa!" Poppy called out. "If I put on my tennis shoes and Daddy says it's okay, I can walk on Main Street."

"Do you want to sort that out?" Morgan asked quietly.

She swallowed. "When I'm done, we're searching the office."

It didn't take long to get Poppy ready, for her to

run down the stairs, filled with excitement over a walk on Main Street. It was hardly surprising that she had taken to Tessa's parents immediately. Her parents had a lot of nurturing to spare.

Once the door shut behind them, Tessa was back in Morgan's office. Glad she'd changed into light khaki pants, she crawled around the perimeter of Morgan's desk. Nothing. Undaunted, she crawled into the space below the middle drawer. She started to withdraw empty-handed when she saw a tiny gleam. Crawling deeper, she retrieved the metal object. Back in the light, she saw that it was a black metal case.

"What's that?" Morgan questioned.

She turned it over in her hand. "I think it belongs to Janet." Tessa opened the case, seeing Janet's name on both cards inside. "I thought so. She said she'd lost the case, thought it was in my office."

"Then how did it get under my desk?" Morgan asked.

"I suspect if we knew that, we'd know about the fate of your survey."

"Are you accusing Janet?" he asked incredulously. "I've known her virtually all my life."

Tessa felt her insides freeze. Her own acquaintance with Morgan was far, far shorter. Did that make her an automatic suspect?

"I'll talk to Janet," Morgan decided.

Immediately Tessa wondered where the survey

was, how much time they had to search before it, too, was sold to the highest bidder.

She lifted her eyes. Morgan's gaze was grim. Faltering inside, she realized he did suspect her. Despite the closeness she thought they had grown to share, he was wondering if she had stolen the survey from him.

The tiny bit of hope she'd been able to cling to that he might come to care for her evaporated. Blindly she looked away, wanting more than anything to simply disappear.

"I'm going to Houston," Morgan announced. "To keep my meeting with the geologist. If—" he paused "—you can watch Poppy for the evening? I may need to stay over, see some people tomorrow, too."

Her voice stolen, she nodded, a jerky movement that seemed unconnected to her. Her heart, too, seemed unconnected. Because if it were still intact, the pain would be crushing, destroying what was left of it. Why did her parents have to be here? If they weren't, she could sling her things into a suitcase and jump into her car, driving away as fast as she dared.

Tears gathered beneath her eyelids, struggled to push past them. But she was resolute, refusing with every bit of her will to let them fall.

Morgan reached for the phone. "I'm going to call Janet."

She wondered if he'd told her as a warning. But

she couldn't ask. She couldn't speak. Turning before he could see that her lips were quivering, her eyes watering, she fled up the stairs.

Chapter Twenty

Alone, Morgan stared after her, his heart so heavy it felt as though he carried a slab of granite in his chest. Maybe that was what his heart would turn into—stone. Slowly he picked up the black card case, turning it so that the light glinted on the dark surface. He hadn't seen it beneath his desk, could have sworn that nothing had been there. Hating the thought, he realized that Tessa could have palmed the case, planting it so that it would appear to be found close to where the survey had disappeared.

But why? Had she and her ex-husband plotted this from the beginning? How, then, had they known there would be an opening, Miss Ellis's position? He thought, too, of Cindy. She had been a good friend to him and also to Lucy. His late wife had been an uncannily good judge of character. She would have soused out a faker in little time. But Cindy had been a favorite friend of hers. Actually, a favorite of his, as well.

But he'd known Janet Divo since school days. And

they had dated. She had always been a kind, good person. What would motivate her to betray him? Money was always high up there in motives. Knowing Janet, if she needed money he would have expected her to ask for a raise, a bonus even, before stealing. She had ferried a survey to Houston—well, actually, she had instructed Sherry to. Tessa had delivered the next one. So what did that prove? That both women, people he thought he could trust, had held the important information in their hands.

Morgan considered the times he had watched Tessa with Poppy, reading her bedtime stories, singing lullabies, soothing her through bad dreams. It didn't fit with a saboteur, someone who had come here for the sole purpose of stealing information.

But he had to admit she couldn't have provided a more effective, more clever cover than insinuating herself into Poppy's life. It didn't take an expert to know how he would regard Poppy's caretaker.

Logic leaped to the forefront. Tessa couldn't have known Dorothy would have a stroke, that Poppy would need to be cared for. And colluding with her ex-husband? Was that in any realm of probability? Not with what she had told Morgan. He thought of Tessa mounted on Beauty, how naturally she sat the mare, how naturally she had fit into his family.

In matters of business, Morgan didn't often question his judgment. He had a knack of ferreting out the truth, finding the downsides of his business deals. But he had crossed into unknown waters with

Tessa. She should have been an able right hand, nothing more. But she was insinuated in every part of his life—with Poppy, Dorothy and Alvin. He didn't dare add himself to that list, not if he was going to keep a calm head.

Taking a deep breath, he hit the button preprogrammed with Janet's phone number.

She picked up on the second ring. "Must be something going on if you're calling me on Sunday. Is Dorothy okay?"

"She's fine. Well, you know, getting better."

"Glad to hear it," Janet replied. "I've been worried about her. Most of my reports have been from Tessa. It's good to hear an update from you. Sorry, you called me. What's up?"

"Found your credit-card case."

She didn't hesitate. "Great! I was beginning to think I'd have to cancel those two cards. You know what a pain that is. Where was the case? Tessa's office?"

"Well, it's kind of odd. It was in the kneehole of my desk, shoved in back."

"Hmm." Janet paused. "I can't imagine how it got there. I spilled my purse in Tessa's office. I thought I got everything, but when I needed to use my debit card at the grocery store I realized I didn't have the case."

Morgan hesitated, hating to question Janet, but knowing he had to. "Did you have any occasion to be at my desk?"

"Actually, I did. Sherry and I were working on some reports. Tessa was on her computer. You were gone and so we used yours. No security risk there, though. Your files are password protected. We could only get to the basics. Hmm." Janet paused again. "I still can't figure out how the case ended up under your desk, though. I didn't have my purse with me at your desk. I left it in Tessa's office."

His stomach sank so low he wondered it didn't drag on the ground.

"Do you want me to pick up the case now?" Janet asked when he didn't speak.

"No." He took a chance. "I'm headed to Houston in a little while, probably be there tomorrow, as well."

"Everything okay?"

No, nothing is okay. "Sure. Sorry I bothered you on Sunday."

"It's never an imposition." Janet paused. "I hope you really know that, Morgan." An unexpected note had crept into her voice.

He remembered Lucy teasing him, telling him that his high school sweetheart was still very much sweet on him. He had always thought it was in fun. Surely Janet didn't have any lingering feelings. They had just been kids then.

He packed a small suitcase. His private office in Houston had a full bath and a perfectly comfortable sofa. He could sleep there and avoid the crush of a hotel.

Pausing, he wondered if it was wise to leave Poppy. But Tessa had never seemed anything but trustworthy with Poppy. And her parents as well as Dorothy and Alvin would be there. Still…

Abandoning his plans for Houston, he rethought what he should do next. Deciding he wouldn't tell Tessa he was staying at home, he regrouped, taking everything he needed up to his room, including his laptop. One place to start was in his correspondence.

First he sent a memo to Tessa asking her to secure the after-hours logs from building security in Houston. He looked up the number she would need to call and included it in the memo. He wondered at the wisdom in letting her have access to the logs. Closing his eyes briefly, he remembered the moments they had shared over the past months. Was she really capable of being a Mata Hari? Could she have faked the tenderness she had shown Poppy? All the many kindnesses he had witnessed?

Tessa would no doubt be confounded by the memo he sent since they hadn't communicated that way since the first days she had begun working for him.

But then the morning would be full of surprises, starting with him being in Rosewood rather than Houston. He phoned the number he had just looked up. Having his own copy of the security logs was imperative.

Tessa tossed back the handmade quilt and soft cotton top sheet. Not having slept even five minutes, she felt ragged. However, her parents were still in town, planning to stay until early afternoon. She couldn't bear to tell them that Morgan suspected she had stolen his confidential information. And little Poppy still needed care. That couldn't continue, though. It was already incredibly painful thinking of saying goodbye to the little one. Although Dorothy wasn't yet ready to care for her, Tessa knew Cindy would come through in a pinch. And she was one of the few people Morgan would trust his daughter with.

Tessa closed her eyes, imagining how her friend would feel when she told her what had happened. Appalled, horrified, upset. She didn't think Cindy would believe her capable of theft, but Morgan was also a friend.

What a ghastly mess. All because she had allowed herself to be taken in yet again. She knew she couldn't pick men, that she couldn't trust her own judgment, yet she had fallen under Morgan's spell, his charm, his appeal. She was a complete and total idiot. It was one thing to be taken in once. But to repeat the process…that took a special kind of stupid.

Dressing quickly, she headed down to her office. She needed to get things together so she wouldn't leave her work in a mess. After turning on her computer, Tessa automatically checked her inbox first, then frowned. An email from Morgan? Not that she wanted to talk to him. Still.

She read the email. Strange request, but she picked up the phone. Since building security was a twenty-four-hour operation, she reached the morning supervisor, who agreed to email the sign-in logs for the Houston office building shortly.

It occurred to Tessa that Morgan wanted to check the day she had delivered the survey to his private office. Funny that he had asked her to handle the request. Didn't he believe her capable of altering the logs? She was surprised he hadn't asked Janet since he had known her since the dawn of time and clearly he trusted her far more.

Realizing her attitude was downright bratty, she swiveled in her chair and left the office, heading for the kitchen. Beating Nancy to the helm was rare, but she had managed. She grabbed the kettle and plugged it in. She needed a cup of bracing tea—English or Irish breakfast. Either would help rid her of the night's exhaustion, the endless hours since she had taken refuge in bed only to find she was torn between tears and unending waves of memories. Neither had been kind.

Tessa knew she had to call on her reserve of strength. It had gotten her through the worst days of her husband's desertion and their subsequent divorce. And she had to stay in Rosewood only until she sorted Poppy's care. Technically, she didn't have to. Poppy was Morgan's responsibility.

A clear, new thought jelled. Maybe this wake-up call was what they both needed. If Morgan was forced to delegate some of his work, he could spend more time with his daughter. Tessa poured boiling water over the tea bag in her cup, then added a dash of honey.

Holding the cup, she let the heat seep into her fingers. The solution for Morgan and Poppy had been staring her in the face the entire time. Morgan needed to have no other choice than to spend time with Poppy. No one like herself or Dorothy to step in and give him an out. It wouldn't be all that long until Poppy was in school. These precious youngest years would be gone.

As would she.

Braced by the tea, she returned to her office. Her email indicated a new message. True to his word, the building supervisor in Houston had scanned the sign-in logs and attached them. Nothing stood out. Well, except the visit by Janet the same night Tessa had delivered the first survey. Printing out the pages, she then highlighted Janet's signature. She put the marked document on Morgan's desk.

Running upstairs, she checked on Poppy, who was sleeping soundly. She stopped long enough to apply some makeup and hide the shadows under her eyes, then pulled her hair back in a loose ponytail.

Nancy had arrived while she was upstairs, and the lovely smell of brewing coffee consumed the dining room. Her parents would be up soon and she needed to entertain them until it was time for their trip down Main Street. She hoped they would pack up first so they could get started on their way home after their walk. She didn't want them dragged into the affair.

Tessa swallowed. How had it come to this? For a blinding moment, she wondered if it had all been a horrible nightmare.

Stepping into the office, she saw the marked document on Morgan's desk. No, it was all too real. Unable to bear being in the room, she turned on her heel and came face-to-face with Morgan. She had to put out her arms to not slam into him.

He extended his arms at the same time and for one ridiculous, mind-numbing moment they were almost in an embrace. Then, as though the gesture could have any meaning, Morgan jerked away. How was she going to get through this day?

"I…" Her voice failed for a moment. "I thought you were going to be in Houston."

"Plans change."

Irony swirled around them like fog off a London dock.

"So they do," she managed, stepping to one side, putting distance between them. "Um, the security logs you wanted are on your desk."

"Did you find anything…out of the ordinary?"

"I highlighted one signature."

He searched her eyes. Tessa desperately wanted to hide the flush of emotions she was feeling. It was horrible knowing what Morgan thought. She couldn't bear having him know her feelings, as well.

Bolting across the entry hall, she headed for the kitchen. Nancy was whipping up her delicious Belgian waffles. Tessa heated the kettle again. Leaning against the counter, she hung on to her mug, needing an anchor. Any kind of anchor.

Morgan studied the building sign-in logs. Tessa had highlighted the same signature he had on his own copy. There was no reason for Janet to have been in his office on a Sunday evening. The same Sunday evening Tessa had gone there to deliver the first survey.

He envisioned both women. Neither seemed a candidate for corporate espionage. But he remembered his father's advice when he had first joined the firm. To never take things at face value, to study and analyze what went on in the business.

Unable to face Tessa's parents, he skipped breakfast, choosing coffee instead. He hadn't slept. Going on little other than caffeine, he was running on fumes.

He had listened all night, not sure what he expected to hear. He had caught Tessa watching over Poppy, tucking in kicked-off covers. Real incriminating.

Exhaling, he wished he knew, really knew, what had happened. Glancing at the clock, he saw that Janet should be in the office. It was time to ask the tough questions. And he wanted to do it in person.

Only ten minutes later, Janet was surprised when he walked up to her desk.

"Morgan! I wasn't expecting you." She smiled and held up her mug. "Coffee?"

He shook his head.

Her smile faded. "Is something wrong?"

Morgan unfolded the security log. "Janet, did you go to Houston one Sunday evening?"

She nodded immediately. "Sure did. Actually, I saw Tessa there. We nearly scared each other to death. I never did find the contract you asked me to pick up."

"I didn't ask you to pick up a contract."

"Yes, you did." She turned to her computer. "I have it in my email." She scrolled down the messages. The confidence in her face edged into a frown. "Well, I don't see it now. I must have transferred it into the departmental correspondence. But I remember because it was unusual. You don't often ask for anything on the weekend, but the times you have it's usually been by phone, not email."

"So you went to the Houston office on that Sunday evening to pick up a contract?"

She nodded. "But I couldn't find it. I put a note to you in the daily folder we delivered the next morning. Surely you saw that."

"No, Janet, I didn't."

Confusion filled her eyes.

Morgan knew he had to ask the difficult questions. "Did you look in the envelope Tessa delivered?"

Janet lowered her gaze. "I was curious. I wanted to know what was so important that Tessa had to deliver it in person. I shouldn't have looked, but I did. It was just a survey."

"Just?"

"I don't remember where the property was." She shrugged. "Just seemed odd that you'd send both of us on an errand that only needed one person."

Morgan didn't know what to think. But he did remember that Tessa kept a reader file, one that contained every interoffice memorandum. If Janet had sent a memo, it should be either in the paper file or in the scanned documents.

He phoned Tessa, hearing her surprise at his request, then agreement.

Replacing his cell, he glanced at the next desk, where Sherry sat sipping her coffee. Maybe she could help, as well. "Sherry?"

She straightened as though just then realizing he was there. "Yes?"

"We're looking for a memorandum from me to Janet." He gave her the pertinent details. "She thinks it could be in the departmental correspondence. I'd like you both to look for it."

Sherry turned to her computer screen and began scrolling through the memos.

Morgan grabbed a mug of coffee and retreated to his office. About thirty minutes later, he reemerged.

Sherry shook her head when he asked if she'd found it. "It's not here. Janet, are you sure it was a memo?"

Janet looked exasperated. "Yes, I'm sure."

"Then it should be here," Sherry replied in a conciliatory tone. "I'll keep looking."

Morgan's cell phone rang. "Yes."

"There's not a memo," Tessa told him. "I looked all through the hard-copy file in case it was misfiled and through all the scanned memos. It's not here."

Morgan clicked off the phone, as uncertain as when he had arrived. It remained one woman's word against the other's. Janet claimed he'd sent her a request to go to the Houston office the same day as Tessa had gone. If that was true, Tessa should have his copy in her useful hard-copy file.

"Sherry, would you bring me the delivery log from the mail room?"

"Sure."

After she left, he suddenly remembered another memo he had sent. "Janet, do you remember about three months ago when I emailed you about the Dunbar contract? I called you, then emailed you the details. I needed the geologist's notes and the original drilling logs. You picked them up in Houston. It was a Saturday, but still a weekend."

Janet nodded. "Yes, I remember."

He picked up his cell phone again. "Tessa, I know your parents are here visiting, but can you bring the hard-copy reader file and a flash drive with the scanned set? Better bring six months' worth."

"What does this other memo prove?" Janet asked.

He rubbed his forehead. "I'm not sure. Look, have some coffee. I'll be in my office."

Janet glanced at her abandoned mug. "Sure."

Spotting Tessa when she arrived, Morgan waved her into his office. "Hard copy or disk?"

"Either," she replied.

He took the flash drive, explaining what they were looking for and the time period.

Only a few minutes passed before Tessa held up a paper. "This looks like it."

Noting the date, he scrolled down until he spotted the same memo.

Tessa trailed behind him as he took the proof to Janet. Then he reconsidered. "Sherry, check the correspondence file."

She nodded, opening that screen again as he gave her the date.

"It's a memo I sent to Janet."

After a few minutes, each of which seemed to contain a thousand seconds, Sherry shook her head. "Afraid not."

"Janet?" he questioned.

She shook her head.

He waited for a moment, meeting Janet's gaze. "No? I have it here." He held up the copy Tessa had given him. He opened his other hand to reveal the flash drive. "And on here."

"I must have missed it," Sherry improvised.

Janet stared from Morgan to Sherry. "Didn't you search by sender and recipient? It has to be there."

Sherry frowned. "Evidently I missed it."

"And you missed the one about me going on that Sunday night, too?" Janet questioned.

"I guess so," Sherry replied.

Tessa stared at the women, then back at Morgan.

He met her eyes, then let his gaze linger on Janet. At last he spoke. "It's not adding up."

Tessa tried to make sense of what he was saying. Then it hit her. No wonder he wanted her to bring the correspondence files. To a neutral location, in front of witnesses. Then bring her together with what he considered the evidence of her leaking information. Tessa was the only one with the memo, so she could be the only one to have betrayed his trust.

Blindly Tessa turned away, trying to navigate the unfamiliar office. Seeing the front desk, she bolted toward it, then down the stairs and outside.

Breath ragged, she yanked open her car door, making her escape. She had to concentrate to keep the car on a steady course, thinking only of getting away.

Arriving at the house, she saw that her parents' car was gone. She slumped her face against the steering wheel. They must have taken Poppy with them on their stroll down Main Street. That would delay her departure.

Tessa rushed toward her cottage. Inside she tried to think of what was hers, what she needed to pack. The sweet French country interior was unchanged. She hadn't left one personal mark. Irrationally, the fact that she'd left no impression, no impact, was devastating. Who would notice in any event? In a year or two, would Poppy even remember that she was once part of her life? Morgan no doubt would spend time trying to forget that she had been.

Spurred on by the thought of him, she rushed from the cottage to the house, heading straight for her office. There she had left somewhat of an imprint. Framed photos of her parents, a snapshot of Poppy, and lying on the desk was the hand-beaded bracelet that Poppy had made for her.

As quickly as she'd run inside, Tessa's energy collapsed. Thumping into her office chair, she reached one shaky hand to pick up the bracelet. She remembered Morgan's grin when Poppy had presented him with a bracelet, too. Tessa had helped her pick out some brown and black stone beads that didn't look feminine. Both of them had been so pleased. Morgan's gaze had gentled and more than appreciation gleamed in his eyes.

Or had she imagined that?

With everything crumbling, she held on to the little beaded bracelet. The tears, always held back so tightly, slipped down her cheeks. She felt a sob in her throat, then jumped when Morgan's hand touched hers.

Mortified, she pulled back, brushing at her tears. "Did you come back to gloat?"

Morgan shook his head. "I couldn't believe it was you or Janet, but it had to be somebody. Then it hit me. Sherry couldn't find the memos. Sherry, who had access to Janet's email, her folders, who could listen to phone conversations. I asked Janet who took that first survey to Houston. She'd trusted Sherry with the errand, even given her an extra day off to compensate for the trip. But it was too neat. Too tidy."

All Tessa could process was how he had suspected her.

"I didn't hire Sherry's husband when Adair closed," Morgan continued. "He wasn't the only one. I couldn't take on their whole workforce. I wondered if Sherry was trying to get back at me."

Tessa stared at him, her breathing uneven.

"Then I looked, really looked, at Janet. It was something in her eyes. I can't explain it, but I knew she was lying. She got the idea from the first memo I'd sent asking her to pick up a contract on a Saturday. She destroyed the memo, which is why it wasn't in her files or the department files. But you had it in the hard-copy file, something she hadn't counted on. And she didn't expect to run into you in the Houston office, which is why she claimed I'd sent her via email. She set it all up—so obviously that I had to believe the leak was either Sherry or you." He met Tessa's eyes. "She was hurt when I hired you instead of promoting her, and then she got angry when she saw that we were getting closer. Said she wanted me to notice her, to remember the love we used to have."

"And did you?"

"We were in high school! A couple of kids. I never loved her like—"

"Lucy," Tessa finished for him, realizing the irony. How had she ever expected to match that sort of love?

"No. I mean yes, I loved Lucy but I need...want to explain why I was so confused. I had a lot of crazy thoughts," he admitted. "When your father told me that your ex worked for United, that Traxton had been bought out by them, for a short...incredible time it seemed plausible that you were responsible."

"Plausible?" The agony made her quiver. "Was it plausible that I cared for your daughter, your house, Dorothy and Alvin so I could steal from you? What was my grand plan? To cause Dorothy's stroke? Then swoop in and raid your company? My ex? What do you know of him? He may not have been an ideal spouse but he isn't a thief, either."

"I know it doesn't make sense." Morgan reached for her arms but she pulled back. "I had a hard time believing it could be Janet. I think you can see why—"

"What I can *see* is that when the chips were down, the first person you suspected was me. Of *stealing* from you. I've been fooling myself, thinking you cared about me, that what I brought to your family meant something." She swiped at the tears that still slipped down her face.

Morgan took a step closer.

"No." She shook her head. "I'm leaving." She

gripped the bracelet tighter. "As soon as my parents get here. I tried to work out how you were going to cope with Poppy when it hit me. Forcing you to be with her is the only way you'll make enough time for her. You've had too many outs already."

"You're upset—"

"Of course I'm upset," she retorted, taking a shaky breath. "I broke all my own rules. I know not to trust, not to believe, but I did anyway. Stupid, I know. Especially when you still don't know everything about me. I'm not a thief, but I kept something from you, something big. It doesn't matter now." Tessa shook the thought of her childlessness away. There would never be a happily-ever-after for her. "I hope for your sake and for Poppy's that you'll find your way back to the Lord, but that's your journey. And you've made it crystal clear that your path doesn't include me."

"Tessa, calm down. Let me apologize—"

"Because your first thought was to suspect me?" The tears subsided and she shook her head sadly. "I'm packing and I'm leaving as soon as my parents get back."

"What about Poppy? How will that make her feel?" Morgan asked desperately. "She couldn't love you more if you were her own mother."

"I'll never be *anyone's* mother." Her voice caught and she put up a clenched hand to stifle a threatening sob.

"Tessa, please."

Since he filled the archway into the larger office, she turned abruptly, escaping through the side door. Tessa knew she couldn't listen to any more excuses. She also knew that between them was a gulf so wide nothing could ford the gap.

Head down, she darted out of what had been her office to the cottage she'd yet to make a home. Engrossed in her own suffering, she didn't see Poppy, who slipped from Morgan's office. Trying to keep just a fraction of her dignity together, Tessa willed herself to become invisible as she retreated.

Chapter Twenty-One

Tessa couldn't think any longer. Her brain felt as though it had passed between two giant presses, squeezing out every last thought. She had to pull herself together. So Morgan no longer believed she was stealing from him. But he had. That was inescapable, which rendered his apology moot. She thought of all the things she had done for and with Morgan and Poppy. She'd actually felt in her heart that they were a family.

Reaching into the closet, Tessa pulled out a suitcase. Weary beyond belief, she tossed the case on her bed, then slumped down beside it.

What was she going to tell her parents? And Poppy? What would she tell her precious girl?

It wasn't fair, she railed inwardly. To taste the fullness of a life she'd always wanted, then... She had been right about one thing, she acknowledged bitterly. Experience hadn't helped her sense of judgment. If Morgan could this easily distrust her, how would he have stood the test of time?

Fool, she told herself. She had fallen for the whole family. How stupid was that? Poppy's sweet face emerged in her thoughts. Not completely foolish. She wouldn't trade her time with Poppy. But Morgan… Would she give back the days with him?

Realizing she was torturing herself with answerless questions, she reached for the suitcase. Once it was open, Tessa began to fill the case with clothes. Not caring how they fared, she stuffed dresses, suits and blouses randomly inside.

A quick knock sounded on her door. Startled, she wondered if Morgan had followed her.

"Tessa?" Sheila called out.

"Mom!" Tessa hustled into the bathroom so her mother couldn't see that she'd been crying. "Come in."

Sheila pushed the door open. "Hi, sweetie. Is Poppy with you?"

Tessa stalled, not trusting her voice for a moment. Holding a towel to her face, she muffled the sound. "No."

Sheila frowned. "She was with us when we got back. Your dad and I picked up a few goodies at the bakery and we put them in the kitchen. I thought Poppy was right next me. But we can't find her."

Tessa froze. "Did you look in her room?"

Sheila frowned. "We called for her through the house, then figured she must be with you."

Tessa emerged from the bathroom.

"Sweetheart, what's wrong?" Sheila asked, seeing the evidence of tears.

"It's nothing, Mom. How long have you been home?"

"A few minutes. Why?"

Heart thumping, Tessa tried to remember each agonizing moment she had been in the house. Would she have heard the kitchen door open and close from her office? Unlikely.

"Did you come in through the front door?"

"Like I said, we picked up some goodies—"

"And put them in the kitchen," Tessa finished dully. "She must be somewhere in the house." Her brain clicked back to life. "She sometimes goes into Morgan's office." A horrid thought was suddenly clear. "Mom, Morgan and I were arguing. Poppy may have overheard."

Sheila searched her face, coming to her own conclusion. "It was bad."

"Mom, we have to find Poppy."

"Of course. I'll get your dad."

"Would you tell Morgan?" Tessa pleaded. "I'll grab Dad."

"Really bad," Sheila muttered. "Of course."

Within a few minutes, the house was alerted. Alvin and Morgan scoured the grounds while Rachel and Nancy helped Tessa and her parents search the house. There were many hiding places in the old house but none of them contained Poppy.

Alarmed, Tessa tried to organize her thoughts. Where would Poppy go? She riffled through memories of the past months. Poppy's all-time favorite place was the city park. Telling her mother, Tessa rushed out to the car. The park was within walking distance but she could drive faster than she could walk. On the way she watched carefully but didn't spot the youngster.

Worry grew as she neared the park. What if Poppy wasn't there? Where else would she have run to?

Reaching the park, Tessa got out, shading her eyes as she scanned the grounds. Not seeing her, Tessa felt her stomach drop.

Suddenly she heard a wail. Not certain where it was coming from, Tessa whirled in a circle. Then she realized the sound was coming from above.

Knowing Poppy's favorite spot was beneath the big oak, Tessa raced across the lawn.

"Help!" Poppy wailed.

Looking up, Tessa saw that Poppy was precariously perched, wobbling. "Hold tight, sweetheart. I'll be right there." Disregarding her fear of heights, Tessa grabbed the lowest limb and began climbing.

Refusing to look down, she kept her movements steady as she navigated through the branches. Fear for Poppy superseded her own anxiety.

Finally reaching the little girl, Tessa plucked her from an unsteady limb, cradling her close. "You're okay. We're going to get down safely."

Poppy clutched Tessa. "Don't let go."

"I won't, sweetheart."

"Uh-huh!" Poppy wailed.

Tessa patted her back. "No."

"You said!"

Trying to understand, the truth suddenly crystalized. Poppy had surely heard her say she was leaving. She wouldn't lie to the girl and say she was staying after all, but she had to say something to calm her down. "We are going to get you down safely. Don't worry about anything else."

Poppy continued crying as she held on to Tessa.

Regret mixed with love and spilled into Tessa's heart. Despite everything, she knew she not only loved this little girl, she loved Morgan, as well. "Let's get you down." Tessa lifted Poppy, setting her securely on the next branch below. As she did, she caught a glimpse of what seemed the distant ground. Instantly shaken, she grabbed the closest limb. Telling herself to get a grip, she avoided looking down again, but the tremors had already begun.

"Tessa! Poppy!" Morgan shouted.

Glancing down, Tessa felt the earth shift. Knowing it hadn't, she broke into a cold sweat. "Come get Poppy," she called down.

Morgan immediately began climbing. Tall and muscular, he sprinted up the big oak, reaching them in no time.

Poppy fell into his arms. "Daddy!"

Morgan sought Tessa's eyes, his own filled with a flush of emotion. "I'll take her down."

Using one arm to secure Poppy, Morgan deftly

used the other to help guide himself down the length of the trunk.

Seeing they were safe, the tight control on Tessa's fear slipped. She closed her eyes, too frightened to look down, too frightened to see beyond this minute. Because they led to a host of tomorrows. Empty tomorrows.

She wavered, shifting just like the leaves in a breeze.

Her head felt light.

"Just let go!" Morgan shouted.

Tessa darted a glance below.

Morgan stood, his feet planted apart, his arms open. "I'll catch you!"

Consciousness was fading, she realized as the cold sweat consumed her.

"Trust me!" he hollered. "Tessa, trust me!"

Could she? Could she ever trust again?

As though conspiring with Morgan, the wind itself pushed her forward. With a whoosh, she released the branch, sliding from the base of the tree.

Expecting to feel nothing, she was startled when hard, firm arms grabbed her, pulling her close.

"Tessa," Morgan whispered in her ear. "Trust me, Tessa. Forgive me."

Could she? Slowly, feeling as though she was awakening, Tessa lifted her gaze.

Morgan's eyes were clear, shadowed only by concern. And, yes, love.

She opened her heart, feeling the quaking only his embrace induced.

"Will you be my love?" he asked, his arms pulling her even closer. "Stay with me, us?"

Her mouth opened, but she grappled with a reply.

"I prayed," he confessed. "When I saw you about to topple. I prayed that you would be safe, that you and Poppy would be safe."

Tears of the good variety prickled, teasing her eyelids open. Tessa swallowed. "Truly?"

"Truly. And He answered."

Poppy pulled on her hand. "Will you be my mommy now?"

Morgan met Tessa's eyes. "Yes, will you?" His lips eased into a hopeful smile.

And Tessa knew her fate was sealed.

Morgan and Tessa read Poppy one last story, sang one last song.

"I talked to Ronnie," Morgan said quietly as they waited for Poppy to drift off. He had joined her midway through the first story.

"And?"

"You were right. He's delighted and he'll move to Rosewood as soon as school is out."

"No worries about the move?"

"No. Longview's gotten pretty rough. He's happy to bring his family here."

"Good."

"And I'll do the same again when I find the next

person," Morgan added. "I'll build a management team. Then I'll always have time for my family."

"What did United say about the oil leases?"

"Since they didn't know Janet was misrepresenting herself, they're backing off, relinquishing their hold on the leases. United doesn't want a lawsuit. The leases will be back in Harper's hands as soon as the attorneys sort out the details."

"Then the company's future is safe?"

"I've given it my all." He met her gaze. "Now it's time to give to the most important people in my life."

"It's still hard to believe Janet went to such lengths," Tessa murmured. "I should have told you I saw her that night in Houston. But things were so crazy with Dorothy and Poppy that I forgot about it."

"Wouldn't have made any difference. She would have come up with a plausible excuse. She was determined to point the blame in your direction," Morgan admitted. "She thought it would be enough to get rid of you. She only included Sherry to have another suspect in case I didn't believe it was you."

"Oh."

Morgan cupped the back of her neck. "But that's not going to happen. Nothing's going to get rid of you."

"I think she's asleep," Tessa said in a near whisper, tucking Freckles close to Poppy.

He nodded, then reached for her hand. "She'll have sweet dreams now that she knows you're staying."

Tessa hesitated, then walked with him out of

Poppy's room. She tilted her head back at the bed. "There won't be any more like her if I stay."

He didn't understand, but kept still.

"It's the reason Karl divorced me. I can't have children," she confessed.

"We already have one," Morgan replied, knowing he could share Poppy with her. "And if we want more, they have this thing called adoption. I hear it works really well."

"Are you certain?" she questioned.

"Utterly. Think of the kids at Cindy's house who need families."

"I don't want to compromise your happiness," she replied quietly.

He tipped up her chin. "The only way you could is if you left. Promise me that will never happen."

Her eyes intensified to that iridescent shade of clear, endless oceans, as though they'd captured a bit of the Caribbean in their depths. "Not as long as you want me."

"Then always." Needing to cement the commitment, he touched his lips to hers, feeling their yielding softness. "I love you."

Her eyelids closed briefly, guarding those jewels. Then she opened them, the treasure chest unprotected. "I never thought I'd be able to tell you…"

"And now?"

"I love you, Morgan Harper."

His lips fused with hers as the words penetrated his thoughts and heart. Joy. Pure and simple.

* * *

Tradition filled their small town, sifted through its consciousness. And settled in the halls of the community church, its pews, its aged and exquisite stained-glass windows. White roses, intertwined with freshly picked bluebonnets, were tied in delicate ribbon and festooned on those well-used pews. Calla lilies filled the vases that rested at the pulpit.

Townspeople gathered inside, then spread to fill the seats, to celebrate the day. To celebrate this union of soul and heart. A much-improved Dorothy beamed, wearing the butterfly necklace Poppy had given her. Alvin sat beside her in the front row along with Morgan's parents. Sheila and Edward had roles to perform in the wedding, but they had become Rosewood fixtures, deciding to relocate and retire alongside their daughter. Sheila was getting the chance to tweak the design of her new dream house, one that would be built soon.

Tessa stared into the mirror of the bride's room in the chapel. Her ivory dress was deceptively simple. Soft silk swirled as it puddled around her feet, a slim silhouette. She hadn't wanted a bouffant, showy gown. Her taste was simpler, her love greater.

Poppy, their flower girl, was outfitted in a sweet floor-length dress that mimicked Tessa's. She had wanted matching mommy and daughter dresses. Again feeling blessed, Tessa had embraced the idea.

Cindy and Sheila were making certain her dress, hair and makeup were perfect. Tessa knew the one perfect thing was the love she and Morgan shared. Like a promise finally fulfilled, she acknowledged.

In moments she would be walking up the aisle. Never dreaming she would have a second chance, Tessa bent her head, giving thanks to the One who was truly responsible for her happiness.

The organ music signaled time for her entrance. Cindy swept up the back of her gown and Sheila patted her hair one last time.

Feeling fully in step for the first time, she took her father's outstretched arm.

The music carried them up the aisle, the fragrant roses lending their scent. Ripened to enhance the fragrance, she thought briefly, even though the sunshine remained outside. The sun shone through the stained-glass windows, scattering multicolored sunbeams throughout the sanctuary. The very air seemed to vibrate with piercing, exquisite, delicate light.

Tessa spotted Morgan.

And she saw the instant he glimpsed her.

Morgan caught his breath. How had Tessa become even lovelier in the space of a day?

Remembering how he had almost lost her, Morgan thanked the Lord again, for giving him the gift of trust. For the gift of this incredible woman who seemed not to know just how very incredible she was. But he knew. She was as rare as the exotic white orchids she carried in her bouquet, orchids complemented by sprigs of bluebonnets, the wild-flowers she loved.

She reached his side, then lifted her gaze to his. He fell into the jewels that were her eyes. There was a brightness to them he'd not seen before. And a promise.

Edward withdrew his arm and Tessa stepped next to him, her place at his side secure. As they listened to the age-old words, uttered the promises that would bind them for life, they never lost sight of each other's gaze. Like a living thing of its own, their gaze spoke of their love, their trust, the gift of new promise.

"You may kiss the bride," the pastor told him.

As though touching an astonishingly fragile blossom, he pressed his lips to hers. The first of endless embraces, Morgan acknowledged gratefully.

"Mrs. Harper?" Morgan held out his hand.

She accepted it, her eyes bright with tears of joy. "Finally…always."

And even the sunbeams dimmed in comparison as they walked down the aisle hand in hand, the glint of their rings echoing the golden hue of their hearts. Hearts forever entwined, forever true.

* * * * *

Dear Reader,

Family is dear to me. Large ones, small ones. They contain our love, the nucleus of our worlds, the support we all count on. For me, Rosewood embodies that sense of family. Friendship, connection, community is offered in abundance.

I hope you'll enjoy this newest journey to my favorite small town. Tessa Pierce has moved to Rosewood to mend her wounded heart. Morgan Harper can't escape his painful past. But together they have a chance. Each needs healing and love. And love is dished up best in a town that personifies the finest in each of us.

God bless.

Bonnie K. Winn

LARGER-PRINT BOOKS!

GET 2 FREE LARGER-PRINT NOVELS PLUS 2 FREE MYSTERY GIFTS

Love Inspired®

SUSPENSE

RIVETING INSPIRATIONAL ROMANCE

Larger-print novels are now available...

REQUEST YOUR FREE BOOKS!
2 FREE WHOLESOME ROMANCE NOVELS
IN LARGER PRINT
PLUS 2
FREE
MYSTERY GIFTS

⁂⁂⁂⁂⁂⁂⁂⁂⁂⁂⁂⁂⁂⁂⁂⁂⁂⁂⁂⁂⁂

HEARTWARMING™

⁂⁂⁂⁂⁂⁂⁂⁂⁂⁂⁂⁂⁂⁂⁂⁂⁂⁂⁂⁂⁂

Wholesome, tender romances

YES! Please send me 2 FREE Harlequin® Heartwarming Larger-Print novels and my 2 FREE mystery gifts (gifts worth about $10). After receiving them, if I don't wish to receive any more books, I can return the shipping statement marked "cancel." If I don't cancel, I will receive 4 brand-new larger-print novels every month and be billed just $5.24 per book in the U.S. or $5.99 per book in Canada. That's a savings of at least 19% off the cover price. It's quite a bargain! Shipping and handling is just 50¢ per book in the U.S. and 75¢ per book in Canada.* I understand that accepting the 2 free books and gifts places me under no obligation to buy anything. I can always return a shipment and cancel at any time. Even if I never buy another book, the two free books and gifts are mine to keep forever.

161/361 IDN GHX2

Name _____ (PLEASE PRINT) _____

Address _____ Apt. # _____

City _____ State/Prov. _____ Zip/Postal Code _____

Signature (if under 18, a parent or guardian must sign)

Mail to the **Reader Service**:
IN U.S.A.: P.O. Box 1867, Buffalo, NY 14240-1867
IN CANADA: P.O. Box 609, Fort Erie, Ontario L2A 5X3

* Terms and prices subject to change without notice. Prices do not include applicable taxes. Sales tax applicable in N.Y. Canadian residents will be charged applicable taxes. Offer not valid in Quebec. This offer is limited to one order per household. Not valid for current subscribers to Harlequin Heartwarming larger-print books. All orders subject to credit approval. Credit or debit balances in a customer's account(s) may be offset by any other outstanding balance owed by or to the customer. Please allow 4 to 6 weeks for delivery. Offer available while quantities last.

Your Privacy—The Reader Service is committed to protecting your privacy. Our Privacy Policy is available online at www.ReaderService.com or upon request from the Reader Service.

We make a portion of our mailing list available to reputable third parties that offer products we believe may interest you. If you prefer that we not exchange your name with third parties, or if you wish to clarify or modify your communication preferences, please visit us at www.ReaderService.com/consumerschoice or write to us at Reader Service Preference Service, P.O. Box 9062, Buffalo, NY 14240-9062. Include your complete name and address.

HW15